I0760417

Nineteen Eighty

THE SEVEN BOOK EVEN

SARAH M. CRADIT

Cover Design by Sarah M. Cradit
Editing by Lawrence Editing

First Edition
ISBN: 978-1-958744-30-7

Publisher Contact:
sarah@sarahmcradit.com
www.sarahmcradit.com

Preface

If you're here, you've made your way through the preceding six books in the series, traversing through the seventies alongside the Deschanel siblings as they stepped into the people they'd become.

1980 is the end of the road. When I mapped this series out, carefully deciding which years mattered most, I kept coming back to 1980 as the natural end point for these particular stories. Not only the bookend of the decade in which the series began, but a pivot point for the world. For culture and music, for politics and belief systems. It was also the year I was born.

Although the series ends as these pages end, these characters lives go on, to varying degrees of happiness and success. At the end of the book, I've included a section titled "Beyond The Seven," where, if you so choose, you can read about some of these experiences in what I consider the bridge period between this series and the next chronological one, The House of Crimson & Clover, which begins almost three decades later. At some point, I may explore these intervening years, but as of this publication, there still exists a quiet gap between the seventies and the aughts, at least where the Deschanels are concerned.

I hope you find the conclusion to this series satisfying, and if it leaves you wanting more, I've left some natural navigation points for you at the end.

Thank you for taking this journey with Charles, Augustus, Colleen, Madeline, Evangeline, Maureen, and Elizabeth.

Also by Sarah M. Cradit

KINGDOM OF THE WHITE SEA

Kingdom of the White Sea Trilogy

The Kingless Crown

The Broken Realm

The Hidden Kingdom

The Book of All Things

Blackwood Cycle

The Raven and the Rush

The Poison and the Paladin

Southerlands Cycle

The Sylvan and the Sand

The Flame and the Forsaken

Guardians Cycle

The Altruist and the Assassin

The Belle and the Blackbird

Darkwood Cycle

The Melody and the Master

The Hand and the Heart

Sceptre Cycle

The Claw and the Crowned

The Duke and the Disciple

THE SAGA OF CRIMSON & CLOVER

The House of Crimson and Clover Series

The Storm and the Darkness

Shattered

The Illusions of Eventide

Bound

Midnight Dynasty

Asunder

Empire of Shadows

Myths of Midwinter

The Hinterland Veil

The Secrets Amongst the Cypress

Within the Garden of Twilight

House of Dusk, House of Dawn

Midnight Dynasty Series

A Tempest of Discovery

A Storm of Revelations

A Torrent of Deceit

The Seven Series

Nineteen Seventy

Nineteen Seventy-Two

Nineteen Seventy-Three

Nineteen Seventy-Four

Nineteen Seventy-Five

Nineteen Seventy-Six

Nineteen Eighty

Vampires of the Merovingi Series

The Island

and more

The Dusk Trilogy

St. Charles at Dusk: The Story of Oz and Adrienne

Flourish: The Story of Anne Fontaine

Banshee: The Story of Giselle Deschanel

Crimson & Clover Stories

Available as a single collection, The Shorts

Surrender: The Story of Oz and Ana

Shame: The Story of Jonathan St. Andrews

Fire & Ice: The Story of Remy & Fleur

Dark Blessing: The Landry Triplets

Pandora's Box: The Story of Jasper & Pandora

The Menagerie: Oriana's Den of Iniquities

A Band of Heather: The Story of Colleen and Noah

The Ephemeral: The Story of Autumn & Gabriel

Bayou's Edge: The Landry Triplets

For more information, and exciting bonus material, visit www. sarahmcradit.com

The Seven in 1980

Children of
August Deschanel (deceased) &
Colleen "Irish Colleen" Brady

Charles August Deschanel, Aged 30
Augustus Charles Deschanel, Aged 29
Colleen Amelia Deschanel, Aged 28
Madeline Colleen Deschanel, Deceased
Evangeline Julianne Deschanel, Aged 26
Maureen Amelia Deschanel, Aged 24
Elizabeth Jeanne Deschanel, Aged 22

For Lizzy

SPRING 1980

NEW ORLEANS, LOUISIANA
VACHERIE, LOUISIANA
CAMBRIDGE, MASSACHUSETTS

Prologue: Irish Colleen and the Seven

Colleen Deschanel, known as Irish Colleen to her family and friends, walked past the faces of her seven children and nine grandchildren, as she did every night of her life. There were more grandchildren on the way, and she sensed the next decade would bring even more. If Irish Colleen had whispered hope back into the Deschanel family with her blessed fertility, then her children had delivered the long, comfortable exhale of relief.

She no longer felt like the young mother who'd been challenged with the upbringing of unusual children. All her babies were grown, and no longer needed her, if they ever truly had. Irish Colleen, only two birthdays from her fiftieth, wondered where the years had gone. Not because her life had not been filled with memories worth making, but because she couldn't recall exactly when she'd begun to feel old.

Forty-eight, going on eighty.

Irish Colleen had hardly been more than a girl when she married a man who was already looking down the barrel of his own twilight, giving him that which he both needed and wanted most: heirs. Seven who lived to maturity, but more pregnancies than she liked to recall now, when it no longer mattered. She'd brought the promise of a future back to the Deschanels at a time when the hope had all but winked out, and for that, she was a hero among them, but that didn't make her one of them. She would always be Irish Colleen, never just Colleen. Always "the help August married," and never August's wife. She'd stumbled, faltered, many times along the way, but by the grace of God, she'd reared the children he so desperately needed, and now they were each living their own lives, most rearing their own babes.

Charles was thirty now and about to become father to his fifth child. The last four, all girls, all of what he'd wanted most. Irish Colleen believed he loved Nicolas, but Charles had always been driven more by his passions than his loves, and his need of daughters, as she saw it, came from a well that had two pockets. They reminded him of his own perceived failures as an older brother to five sisters, and also of the daughter he would never know, because Irish Colleen had seen to it that his dalliance with a teenager didn't ruin his life. She'd never know if that decision had been the right one, but she was certain he'd have none of these babies if the first had lived.

If she had one regret, it was forcing him into a marriage with Cordelia. His misery traveled the only way it could when it rolled off his icy wife, toward his son. And while Irish Colleen had offered, many times, to raise Nicolas herself... to give him the nurturing he deserved, and that, perhaps, she hadn't given enough of to Charles... while she'd made this offer in earnest, he'd refused it in equal seriousness. Nicolas was his son, and the sooner he learned to harden himself, the more capable he'd be of existing in an unfair world.

She wanted to ask Charles, her spoiled, tempestuous baby, what *he* could know of an unfair world, born with gold spoons hanging from his pouty lips, but she understood that he'd seen his own share of pain. Some invited, some not.

Augustus thrived as a father. As time went on, he learned to wade in deeper waters, to take more risks. To let Ana fall and scrape her knees, and sting herself on the beautiful roses in his garden. She was a lovely child, full of life, but also so much like her father. Quiet, introspective. But Elizabeth couldn't help him forever. She had her own life to lead, and Augustus' careful balance of work and fatherhood hinged on the constancy of her presence over the past five years.

Irish Colleen had an idea of how she could help her son, but he would need to come to her first. There was a question only he could ask. He'd never appreciated, or followed, unsolicited advice.

And he would. Come to her. This she knew, in her own unique form of magic known as mother's intuition.

Unlike Charles, who seemed thrilled by the idea that his mistress might continue to produce child after child to please him, Augustus insisted one was all he'd ever want. Charles' quest for joy and perfection was never-ending. In Ana, Augustus had found his absolution alongside his happiness.

Colleen had, more and more, been talking about moving back to New Orleans. Her little family unit, now five strong, had thrived in the damp lowlands of Scotland, but the frequent travel home to oversee the Deschanel Magi Collective was taxing, and Amelia would be going into pre-school soon. Noah was preparing to defend his doctoral thesis, and Colleen had a decision to make, about where she'd pursue hers.

While Irish Colleen had been eager to see her namesake run off into the world to find herself, as a woman separate of the family she seemed determined to live and die for, she was just as eager to have her coming back home now. Home, where she could love on her grandbabies, Amelia, Benjamin, and little Ashley. Where, perhaps, she could even have tea with her daughter, woman to woman, and enjoy their relationship in a way age and circumstances had never previously allowed.

Evangeline, in her typical fashion, had quietly finished her graduate program, and just as quietly decided not to return home. She said she was entertaining job offers, but hadn't landed on one, and had nothing pushing her to do so with expediency. Over the years, Irish Colleen had learned to interpret her daughter's calm lack of enthusiasm for something other than apathy, but it didn't mean she understood it. It didn't mean she understood Evangeline, her only child who had *not* met someone to settle down with. At twenty-six, she seemed in no hurry to do so, despite that her best childbearing years were behind and not ahead.

She'd brought that woman home last Christmas. Cassie. Irish Colleen knew Cassie was just a friend, but she also knew there were other women that Evangeline had dated and even loved. This flew in the face of what Irish Colleen believed to be right and true, but she was less concerned with the sin and more with the possibility Evangeline might never carry her unusual way with the world down to others.

Irish Colleen had spent years not understanding Evangeline, but only now was she beginning to accept that she didn't need to. She wanted only to be a part of her child's life, not to mandate the path.

Maureen was finally pregnant with her second child, but that didn't warm Irish Colleen's heart. Not at all. To the opposite, Irish Colleen was quite sure her daughter hadn't renewed her husband's interest in the marital bed, so it could only mean one thing.

There'd been rumors, of course, over the years. She'd heard the name LaViolette bandied about, but never more than a whisper, and Edouard, despite his many faults, had been a good father to Olivia, who had just celebrated her sixth birthday and was every bit the ball of fire her mother had been at that age. He doted on her, even if he neglected her mother. And to hear him talk about the coming child, one would never know it wasn't his.

But he knew. Everyone knew.

Irish Colleen began her descent down the stairs of Magnolia Grace. They'd had Olivia's party there earlier, and she decided to stay the night. She told Augustus she'd take Anasofiya to Montessori in the morning.

"Nana?"

At the top of the stairs, Irish Colleen saw a shock of red hair running rampant around a pale face. "What are you still doing up, sweetheart? You have school tomorrow."

"What are you still doing up, Nana?"

"I'm old, and old people sometimes forget to go to bed."

Ana scrunched her face. "You're not *that* old. You don't have wrinkly wrinkles, or... or..."

Irish Colleen didn't have the slightest idea where her granddaughter was going with this, so instead she swept Ana into her arms and peppered her cheeks with kisses, set to the sweet sound of the little one's giggles. She was tall for her age, but otherwise reminded Irish Colleen of her deceased mother, Ekatherina. Lean. Beautiful. Haunted.

Yet, she also looked like her great-grandmother, a woman she'd never know. Irish Colleen's mother, Enid, who was long gone, but now lived on behind the eyes of a smiling child who was four and a half, going on forty.

"Want me to read you a story?"

Ana shook her head. "I can read my own stories now."

"Oh!" Irish Colleen pretended to be surprised. "Can you now? You're such a big girl. My apologies."

Ana shrugged against her chest, yawning. "It's okay."

"I'm going to take you back to bed. Is that all right?"

"I suppose."

"You sure you don't want me to read to you?" Irish Colleen asked as she settled Ana back under the pile of plush covers.

Ana's soft face spread into a grin. "Okay, Nana, maybe just one." She rolled her eyes to the ceiling, thinking. Across the room, Augustus had set up a bookshelf with hundreds of books, and Ana knew every last one by heart. "The one about the cow who can drive, but is really bad at it and runs over everything."

Irish Colleen laughed. "Not so unlike your nana!"

THIRTY MINUTES LATER, IRISH COLLEEN, EXHAUSTED but contented, left her granddaughter's room. She passed by

Augustus', but his door was closed and his soft snores carried into the hall. Farther down was the room Elizabeth and Connor shared on the nights they still stayed at Magnolia Grace, but Connor had gone home to feed their puppy, Atticus.

Elizabeth wasn't in her room, though. She stood at the end of the hall, looking out the big circular stained glass window that often reminded Irish Colleen of a Catherine wheel.

"Lizzy?"

"Mama," she replied without turning.

"What are you doing?"

"Thinking."

"About?" Irish Colleen approached carefully. A damp chill passed through her as she recalled that it was about the right time of year for their annual tradition. The one that invariably drove a deeper wedge between them, but also, somehow, drew them closer together. Silent conspirators in a dangerous game.

"The usual," she replied, in the voice of a woman. She was almost twenty-two, and had she gone to college with Connor, she'd be receiving her degree this spring.

"Anything you want to share?"

Irish Colleen winced, expecting a dose of Elizabeth's cutting sarcasm as she whipped around to deliver it. Instead, she turned and smiled. There was little joy in the gesture, but there wasn't as much pain as she was used to seeing, either. "Connor wants us to pick a date. He has his heart set on a big wedding."

"You don't." It wasn't a question.

Elizabeth shook her head. She leaned back on the small desk nestled in the nook below the window. "I wish I could wave a magic wand and have it be done. For all our magic, *this* would actually be useful..."

"Lizzy." Irish Colleen chose her words carefully. "You know I'd love to see you in a beautiful gown, surrounded by your favorite flowers, and all our loved ones, and—"

"Mama—"

"But more than that, I wish for your happiness. Why not go

before the judge?"

Elizabeth's smile faded from surprise. "You'd disown me."

"I suggested it, didn't I?"

"Connor has a big Catholic family, too. They have expectations."

"Heavens, dear, are you marrying Connor or are you marrying five hundred Sullivans?"

Elizabeth dropped her gaze to the floor with a small laugh. Her dark blond hair fell around her bony shoulders. She'd lost more weight than Irish Colleen was comfortable with, and the effect made her seem taller, older.

"Ten years ago, perhaps on this very day, you told me one of the seven would die," Irish Colleen ventured. Her voice hitched. "In those ten years, so much has changed. You've changed."

"So have you," Elizabeth replied.

"Yes," Irish Colleen answered. "I have. We all have. And we've had good and bad years in between, but I never want another one like 1970, Lizzy. If that means you never tell me again what you've seen..."

Elizabeth tucked her hair behind one ear. "You won't lose a child this year, Mama. Not that I've seen."

Irish Colleen nearly sagged from the relief of this, and until Elizabeth said the words, she hadn't realized her own had been a question.

But the relief was short-lived, for she could never turn back time to a point where she hadn't overheard sweet Elizabeth tell her sister Colleen that she, Lizzy, would die young. She'd not said when, or how, but that fear would linger over Irish Colleen for the rest of her days, whatever God saw fit to give her. The fear, also, that she might not live to try and prevent it.

Elizabeth did something surprising then. She leaned in to embrace her mother.

"Every year is good, and every year is bad, Mama. Sometimes it's better not to know what the next storm will bring, or when it's coming."

CHAPTER 1

Comfortably Numb

Elizabeth wandered around the party, a flute of half-drunk champagne dangling through her fingertips.

She should have had the presence of mind to plan this. She was Connor's fiancée, the person closest to him above anyone else in the world, even his twin brother, Thomas. Today was a big deal for both brothers, but especially Connor, who would take his new fancy bachelor's degree and enter law school at Tulane in the fall, like so many other Sullivans had before him, and would after.

Thomas decided to buck Sullivan tradition and go on to medical school, which earned smiles and pats on the back, but with decidedly less energy. To their credit, the Sullivans tried to embrace this "defection," putting on an overabundance of saccharine display for his benefit, but they weren't fooling anyone. Thomas could be the next President of the United States, and they'd still whisper that he could've made *such* a promising lawyer.

But both brothers had that day walked with the many other students who'd earned the right to call themselves educated, while Elizabeth had waved from the sidelines, crying tears of pride. Tears of... something else. It wasn't quite regret, because there wasn't a single day that went by where Elizabeth regretted her decision to pull back from the world. But there was a tickle there, of what might've been, what *she* could've been, if not for who she already was.

She wondered if there was a fire code violation at Colin Sullivan Sr.'s Victorian off St. Charles. There must be at least two hundred Sullivans walking the property, inside and out, meandering the tight halls and wild gardens. Although it meant more minds and thoughts to drift her way, more visions to cipher, it was also a nice way to claim she'd gotten lost. When anyone asked later where she'd been, she could wave her hands and talk about how crowded the whole thing had been.

"Sweetie," Connor whispered in her ear. A whiff of whiskey wafted across the humid summer air, burning her nostrils. He was drunk, but that was okay. He never got drunk, and today, he'd earned it.

"Darling," she said, half-teasing, as she turned to kiss him. "Are you enjoying your party?"

His sloppy grin and heavy-lidded eyes gave her all the answer she needed. But he said also, "It feels good. I didn't imagine myself here four years ago."

"Come on. Your grades never dropped once."

Connor waved his hand around. "Not this. I knew I'd graduate. I had no other choice. That's life, right? We make a choice and commit to it."

Elizabeth's smile faded. "I don't understand."

He pressed his forehead to hers, and she got another whiff of the booze. "Lizzy. I love you so much. Today is about futures, and I can't help wishing today was the start of another part of my future."

Elizabeth knew what he meant. She silenced his next words with a kiss, and then said, "I'm so proud of you, Connor. So, so proud. But all these people... I'm struggling today. I didn't want to tell you, because this is *your* day. But if we have a wedding, that will be *my* day as well, and I don't want my joy drowned out by horrible visions. Already today I've seen that one of your cousins is having an affair that will be exposed soon and will rip their whole family apart, and another is unaware of a terminal cancer diagnosis coming in a few weeks." She laced her hands through his clammy ones. "I want to be your wife. In my heart, I already am. Have been for a long time."

Connor sighed and dropped his head. "But not like this."

"Not like this."

Colin and Catherine Sullivan stepped up to give their congratulations. Elizabeth and Catherine exchanged a look as Colin launched into a brotherly speech about what Connor could expect in law school, and later at the firm.

Catherine moved to Elizabeth's side, sipping from her wine glass. "You look so grown, Elizabeth. What are you now, twenty-one, twenty-two?"

"Twenty-two, soon." Elizabeth gave her an odd look, tinged with a smile. "I'm not sure how to take that."

"It's a compliment." Catherine emptied her glass and set it on a nearby table. "Take it like that."

"All right." Elizabeth set her own glass to the side. She didn't like champagne. It had just been a way to keep her hands busy. "How are your kids?"

Catherine blanched. "Kid. Just one."

A pit landed square in the middle of Elizabeth's stomach, as if punched. This was the other real downer of visions. Sometimes she forgot that just because something had already come to pass didn't mean everyone knew. Those who knew Rory and Carolina's daughter, Robyn, was really the result of an illicit affair between Catherine and Elizabeth's brother, Charles, was a small list. One Elizabeth wasn't supposed to be on.

"Right. Sorry," Elizabeth whispered. "Oz. How's Oz?"

"Oz is fine. He's with his grandmother today," Catherine said, but was already angling her body away, eyes searching the crowd for someone else to make small talk with.

Someone who wasn't as weird and damaged as Elizabeth.

. . .

AUGUSTUS CLAPPED CONNOR ON THE BACK, AND THEN, in a move awkward for both of them, pulled him in for a quick half-embrace.

"I'm proud of you," Augustus said. He kept one eye on Anasofiya, who ran and played nearby with Oz and Amelia. He presumed it was some version of tag, as she bobbed and weaved through the flower-laden gazebo, red hair flying, all legs. "You have a bright future ahead."

"Thanks, Augustus." Connor dropped his eyes to his feet. "I appreciate you coming today."

"Are you kidding? I wouldn't have missed it." Augustus cleared his throat. "You're like a brother to me." *More so than my own, at times.*

Connor flushed.

"In every way. Sometimes I'm proud. Sometimes you annoy me..."

They laughed together.

"Any plans for the summer?"

Connor looked past him, and Augustus knew who he was searching for. He'd seen his baby sister wandering around, looking for places to hide in plain sight. He also knew how it pained her to do it, on Connor's special day.

"Not really."

Augustus nodded slowly. He slipped an envelope into Connor's suit jacket and clapped his hand over the spot. "Take Elizabeth somewhere. Not to Baton Rouge, or Destin, I mean somewhere away. Far from here. Europe. Africa."

Connor started to reach for the envelope, but Augustus stopped him. "It's money. My gift to you, and an investment in your future. That will pay for at least the summer away, anywhere you want to go."

"But—"

"You want to marry my sister," Augustus said. "But she won't make it through a day like today. You know that. Take her somewhere… inspiring. I don't have ideas, Connor, this isn't my area of expertise. Last time I tried to take a woman somewhere…" He cleared his throat again. "Anyway, your family will get over it. Mine will get over it. But Lizzy wouldn't get over a big wedding. Take her somewhere and marry her, where it's just the two of you."

Connor exhaled through a small gap in his lips. "Wow. Thanks, Aggie, I don't know what to say."

"It's not about what we say, Connor," Augustus said, clapping him on the back once more. "It's about what we do." As he walked away, he added, "Congratulations again, brother."

COLLEEN SLIPPED HER ARM THROUGH AUGUSTUS' AS they watched their children play in the garden. She remembered a time, not so long ago, when the two of them had played like this. Augustus lost his playfulness by the time his age entered double digits, but when he was young, his imagination was bigger than all of them.

"Ana is getting so tall."

He nodded. "And Amelia. Where do you think she gets that white hair from, anyway?"

"There's a few of us still. Luther is one. But if you look at old photos, it's a trait from long ago that didn't make it into the present day for some reason. We think Ashley's hair might stay that color, too, but we won't know for sure until he's a little older."

"Redheads aren't that common either, I suppose," he replied, nodding at Ana. "Mama said you might be moving back this summer."

"We're seriously considering it," she said, crossing her arms over her chest as she smiled at Amelia. "Do you like Ana's Montessori?"

"Very much. More importantly, she does. Every night when I come home, she has a thousand stories to tell me."

"Has she made many friends? You said before you were worried she preferred being alone."

Augustus waved enthusiastically at his daughter, who was hanging half upside down from the side of the gazebo as if swinging from a tall building. "She prefers to hang out with Nicolas and Oz. Elizabeth tried arranging playdates with some of the mothers of other young girls in her class, but it didn't work out."

"Well, she'll have Amelia soon, too, if everything comes together." Colleen looked up at him. "She looks like you, you know. I know you think she resembles Ekatherina, and I see it, in some ways, but mostly I see you. And Dad."

Augustus twisted his mouth and looked away, into the crowd of partygoers. "Have you talked to Charles?"

"He didn't come today?"

"No."

She shook her head. "I expected I'd see him at Sunday dinner, at Mama's. Why? Is everything okay?"

"I don't know. Nicolas was spending more and more time with us, and sometimes staying a week or more at Colin's. Charles is so wrapped in his girls he doesn't even have time for his son anymore. But now he's pulled back on that and insists Nicolas stay at home. He's all over the place, as always, and Nicolas is the one who suffers. That's nothing new, as you know, but Nicolas is older now, and he's starting to ask questions. Ones I don't have answers to."

"I suspect Charles' motivations are more complex than we give him credit for," Colleen said, but left it at that. Nicolas didn't deserve the treatment he'd been given by his own father, and he was better off with Augustus and Colin. But inwardly, she sighed. Yet another reason she should come home. Another family problem nagging at her from across the sea that she couldn't even begin to help solve unless she was here. "I'll take him, too, when I'm back. Nicolas has no shortage of family who loves him."

"You sound fairly convinced. About coming back."

Yes, she was. So was Noah. But she was also loathe to surrender the magic of Scotland, where she and her husband and their three babies had thrived in ways they couldn't have done had they spent the past five years here, instead.

But everything had a season.

"I'm surprised Maureen didn't come," Augustus said. "Would have been good for her. For Liv. They don't get out much anymore."

Colleen laughed. "She used to fool around with Thomas. She's a new woman now. I'm guessing she didn't need the reminder."

Augustus balked. "No way."

"I guess we're lucky Charles never found out about *that* one."

"Don't even joke about that, Leena," he said, but was smiling.

"I see Connor, but where's Lizzy?"

Augustus turned to his sister with a serious look. "You know why today is hard for her. I'm sending Connor and Elizabeth away for the summer, and I've encouraged Connor to elope with her, wherever they go."

"Elope!"

"Colleen, I need your support on this. Do you want Lizzy's special day to be clouded by horrors she can't control?"

Colleen's mouth flapped open, closed. She didn't know what to say, but whatever words she had were clamped down by her better judgment. Augustus was right. Elizabeth had suffered her whole life, and she deserved this. She deserved to be happy. Her right to that happiness superseded their expectations of her. "What about you? Won't you need help with Ana?"

Augustus turned back to where the kids played. "She's almost five, going on fifty. Sometimes I think she's the one raising me."

Colleen smiled. "She's an old soul. But if you need help, Aggie, I should be back—"

He held up a hand. "I know. But this will be good for us. For Ana and me. When Lizzy comes back married, I'm going to find a way to tell her I don't need her help the way I used to. She needs to focus on starting her own family. I won't be her reason for stagnating."

"She wants to help you, you know. It's not an obligation."

"I know that. But I don't want Elizabeth having any more excuses not to live, Colleen. She has a life ahead of her, and it's time she start embracing it. The rest of us have. It's her turn."

ELIZABETH SWAYED, HUMMING ALONG TO PINK FLOYD as she tidied up the living room. Connor was neater than she was. Hell, anyone was neater than she was. Elizabeth's outside life was just as chaotic as what was inside, and now that she and Connor had a place that was just theirs, she wanted to do better. For him, but also for herself.

She couldn't shake the feeling she'd let him down. He spent so many little moments of *his* day, checking on her, doing little things to make her comfortable. On days like today, Elizabeth could disappear in her never-ending sorrow of inadequacy. She could forget he loved her and wonder why he should at all. She imagined a future with him married to a woman who wasn't constantly struggling uphill.

The door opened and closed. Atticus' tiny paws against the wood floors echoed across the small apartment, followed by Connor's heavier steps. A clatter of metal as he dropped his keys on the small table across from the door.

Elizabeth was suddenly nervous, and she didn't know why.

"That was a long walk," she commented, and then chided herself. She wasn't that kind of girlfriend. She had nothing to suspect anyway. Not from Connor.

"Yeah," he replied. He reached into his pocket and dropped an envelope on the table. "Go on. Open it."

"What is it?"

"There's a very simple, yet effective, way to find out."

Elizabeth rolled her eyes. "If it's a gift, on *your* day—"

"It is a gift," Connor replied, grinning. "But not from me."

Elizabeth approached the table with some trepidation. The nerves were back, and again, she couldn't identify their source. It was as if she and Connor were still courting, and not nearly a decade into their relationship.

"Go on," Connor said, wearing the look of an eager child.

With a heavy inhale, Elizabeth peeled back the unsealed flap. Two plane tickets fell out.

Paris.

"What..."

"A gift from Augustus," Connor explained, in a rush, as if afraid if he took too long she might jump down his throat. "Well, he gave me cash, but it was specifically to take you away for the summer, and, um, I walked down to the travel agency with Atty, you know the one down on, uh, Canal, and, uh, Burgundy, and I realized I didn't *know* where I wanted to take you, but, um, I knew it needed to be special, because the thing is, Elizabeth, I intend to elope with you, across the world somewhere, where it's just us and you're safe, and we're safe, and you can be my wife and we can be happy, and, uh, the travel agent lady suggested there'd be no better place than the City of Lights, which I guess is what they call—"

Elizabeth launched herself at her fiancé, flying into his arms and tangling her own around his neck as she answered the unasked question with tear-stained kisses.

CHAPTER 2

Ready or Not

Tiny footsteps echoed down the marble halls of The Gardens. Luther's brows kept rising and falling with every loud thud, as if expecting a million-dollar vase to come careening to its death in dramatic response. Colleen just laughed. As a mother of three, she was used to not reacting until the vase *did* careen to its death.

"Josephine is so lovely. I'm so happy for the two of you," Colleen said. Luther, now a grown man of eighteen, had married his high school sweetheart over Christmas. She'd come to the wedding, but hadn't had the time to socialize, and so meeting Josephine over tea today had been a nice chance for Colleen to get to know the young woman who'd married her greatest ally on the Council. "And children?"

Luther's cheeks flushed. "We're hoping for a few. Josephine comes from a family even bigger than mine. I think she'll be a wonderful mom."

"And you'll be a wonderful dad," Colleen said, smiling. Amelia came staggering into her legs, nearly knocking her sideways. She wrapped her tiny body around both limbs. "Oof. Where's Ben?"

"Hiding. He thinks I don't know where, but I *do.* He's not so smart."

"Oh, I see." Colleen grinned at Luther, who winked. "And Ash?"

"Daddy took him for a walk in the stroller."

"You didn't want to go?"

Amelia scrunched her face. She whipped her white-blond hair behind her. "I'm not a *baby,* Mom."

"My mistake."

Amelia lifted her face and screamed, "Ready or not, here I come!" and then went peeling off in the direction she'd come.

"She has Noah's mischief in her," Luther remarked.

"She's an interesting child. She can play hard, but then wants to be left alone for hours."

"Has she come into her abilities yet?"

Colleen sighed. She looked down the hall where her oldest had returned to her play. "I think she might be an empath, Luther."

Luther opened his mouth to say something, but then instead just nodded.

"I can't help but make comparisons to Maddy."

Luther touched her arm. "Colleen, you can't make those comparisons. It's not fair to you, or to Amelia. Sometimes who we are, as people, makes the gifts we're given easier, and sometimes it makes them harder. We never know how the combination will work out."

"She's broody, like Maddy."

"Is she? Or are you imagining it, because you're scared?"

Colleen almost jumped down his throat for the presumption, but it was Luther saying this, not someone who didn't understand her. Though a full decade younger than her, he'd become one of her most trusted friends. She often forgot she was the older of the two. "She likes her alone time."

"So do you."

"She's four."

"What were you like at four?"

"I don't remember."

"Well, I can't imagine you were very different than you were at fourteen, or twenty, or twenty-eight."

"I appreciate that you're trying to keep me from worrying," Colleen said. "But we both know the struggles of growing up in this family. Of trying to have normal lives while bearing the name Deschanel. And on top of that... healers, empaths, illusionists."

"There will always be risks. But when we know that, we can help protect our loved ones. Prepare them."

Colleen nodded, thoughts drifting to just how much had changed since she brought Luther onto the Council, a young man barely in high school.

Their beloved Pierce had died in 1977 of an unexpected heart attack, at fifty-one. Pansy and Kitty hadn't been the same since, and neither had the Council, which had always benefitted from his calm hand and open mind. And though Colleen had been eyeing Evangeline for the next open spot, she instead gave it to Jasper Broussard, Cassius' son, to show she wouldn't capitalize on their terrible grief.

But then, good to her word, Eugenia had also stepped down. The death of her half-brother had been the final push, and when she did, Colleen made her move to finally bring Evangeline into the fold.

Cassius would be the next to retire from family work. He was already hinting at it. Colleen wasn't ready to lose him, too, and if and when he did, she had no one in mind to replace him. Her brothers wanted nothing to do with the Magi Council, Maureen was a mess, and Elizabeth... well, Elizabeth did all she could to normalize her condition. This would only bring a finer point on it.

If Colleen looked back a decade, the reflection was even more bizarre. In 1970, she was dating Rory, whom she'd loved but was not in love with, daydreaming of nothing more than the years of college ahead of her, safe in the comfort of her great-aunt Ophelia's tutelage. Now, she'd married a man who she was utterly and irrevocably in love with, and had borne him three children. And now it was she, and not Ophelia, running the august council for the family. Colleen was the one doling out the wisdom and making the hard decisions.

Except, not today. Today, she was reminded the words of another could be even more powerful than the truths within.

"Thank you, Luther," she said and pulled him in for a quick embrace. "I've made some questionable decisions over the years, no doubt, but bringing you in at my side on the Council was not one of them. I'm proud of the man you've become."

Later that night, Colleen dictated her notes from the Council meeting of two days prior to the recorder in her hand, while Noah rocked a sleeping Ashley, glasses perched on his nose, reading *National Geographic.* It was from earlier in the year, January, she thought, because it was the one with Jupiter on the cover. She had her subscription sent to The Gardens, because it gave the two of them something to look forward to on their quarterly visits home for her Council meetings. And not just the two of them... Amelia *devoured* the magazines, disappearing into her room for hours with a stack. Colleen supposed this was why Noah was stuck with January.

How she loved her husband. How *proud* she was of him. He'd successfully finished his doctoral program and was now Dr. Jameson. She'd be next, but more and more, she knew her own degree would come from New Orleans, not Edinburgh.

She clicked the pause button.

"That a good one?" she asked quietly, so as not to wake two-year-old Ashley. She already knew the answer. She'd read it cover to cover herself.

"Oh, yeah, this one's just full of good stuff," Noah said, pushing his glasses back and carefully folding the magazine on the side table. “We should really take the kiddos to Utah. Looks beautiful.”

“We could,” Colleen said. “It would be easier to do it from here, of course.”

Noah pressed his lips together, in a smile that was almost indulgent. “It’s not me you need to convince, dear.”

No, she supposed not. It had never been Noah. He would have left Edinburgh after Amelia was born, had Colleen felt it was the right time. But it wasn’t. Not then.

“It’s tough,” she confessed. “Our babies are thriving there. *We* are thriving there.”

“Our babies would thrive here too. We would thrive anywhere, Colleen. You know that.”

“My family…” Where to start, though? He knew they were odd. He knew they were challenging. And he knew they had problems. Didn’t every family? He even knew her tendency to take everyone’s burdens onto herself. But he wasn’t worried. So why should she be?

Noah shifted Ashley to his shoulder. “Your family has changed without you. And you’ve changed without them. You might even find it easier, because of those changes. Less likely to sacrifice yourself for the cause.”

Colleen dropped the recorder on top of the leather-bound notebook. “Summer, then.” It would give her the time needed to apply and be accepted for the doctoral program at Tulane.

Noah smiled wider. “Summer, then.”

AUGUSTUS KICKED THE SOCCER BALL ACROSS THE YARD. Ana, bounding back and forth across an invisible goal, pulled her tongue between her teeth, challenging him with her eyes.

He didn’t know where she got this moxie of hers. Certainly not from him. Maybe not even from Ekatherina, as he’d never seen that much personality come from her in the short few years he’d known her.

But for all of Ana's boundless energy and competitive spirit, there were other times where he *did* see her mother coming through. In the times where she shrank in the shadow of the young girls who could have been her friends. In the long hours she spent reading books above her age level, curled up in her bed, happily alone.

"You lose!" she cried, sticking her tongue out, joy flashing in her eyes, as she blocked the goal and lifted the ball over her head, chucking it back to him from her tiny hands. It only made it halfway, and when Augustus went to retrieve it, she was quicker, and ran it back to her side, claiming now it was her turn to score on him. "Ready or not, here it comes!"

He didn't really understand the sport. He'd run track for a couple years, and even cross-country, but Augustus had always had bigger priorities. Running wouldn't start his business. It wouldn't turn it regional, and then global, blowing it up beyond his wildest dreams.

And now his business *was* global, and he had everything he'd ever wanted, and more. Ana was the light in his life, and Deschanel Media was the backbone holding this world he continued to create for her in solid form. Though he was nearing thirty, she kept him young and reminded him that sometimes progress came in smaller forms. Sometimes joy could be finding a smooth rock down at the coast, or planting something in the garden with your daughter and watching it grow.

He couldn't take full credit for Ana's development. Elizabeth had been a godsend over the past nearly five years, and so had Colleen, when she was home. Maureen often popped in when she was taking Olivia to the park to see if Ana wanted to come. Ana, though lacking in a real live mother, didn't want for maternal love. As far as Augustus was concerned, Ana had the best aunts on the planet.

But it was time for Elizabeth to live her own life. If all went well, she'd come back from Paris married, and with a new direction in life. Whatever she decided, Augustus would support her, always. But he knew her future wasn't living part-time in his house, helping to raise his daughter, either.

He was so lost to his thoughts he realized she'd scored on him —landing it in the tangle of bougainvillea wrapping the porch— and now it was his turn again.

"Daaaaaaad! Kick the balllllll!"

He could do this alone, and now, it was time to try.

Augustus smiled at his daughter and kicked the ball.

"I just wish you could've come," Evangeline was saying, stretching the phone cord across three different rooms as she haphazardly tossed clothes, shoes, and everything else into her suitcase. "I miss you."

"I miss you too. But you'll be back in New Orleans with your family, soon, and you'll forget all about me being unable to make it up to Boston," Cassie said from the other end. "And CERN! Evie! How many people do we know who can say they're going to work for the European Organization for Nuclear Research?"

"None," Evangeline replied. Despite that MIT was an obvious candidate pool for the esteemed organization in Switzerland, she was the only one from her program who'd been extended an offer. Over the years, she'd changed her focus from neuroscience to nuclear, with the escalating Cold War at the heart of it. If her experience with assault had taught her anything, it was that the worst feeling she had ever known was helplessness. She had no heart for politics, but she could understand the science; could help prepare the world for what might one day be a reality.

But nuclear physics was more than a weapon. It was a way to power the world. It was energy. Life.

Just like the Second Line Foundation, that she and Cassie had established three years ago for survivors of sexual assault. It wasn't therapy. It was encouragement. It was a reminder you could survive and have a whole life ahead of you. That what happened to you was one ring, not the whole trunk. It was stories of survival. A safe place.

"Colleen especially will be so proud of you."

"Yeah. Maybe. I missed our last Council meeting, and I don't think she's happy about that. She doesn't know yet I'll probably miss the next one." Evangeline's hesitation didn't come from her nervousness about her sister's reaction, but from Cassie herself. Something had been amiss with her best friend now for a couple months, and anytime Evangeline asked, Cassie blew it off as Evangeline being over sensitive with graduation looming. Later, she said it was because Evangeline hadn't bothered to invite her family out, which was true, but also not the problem.

"If anyone understands, it's Colleen," Cassie insisted. "When do you move?"

"June. If I take it."

"You will."

"You're so sure of that, are you?"

"Maybe I'll come with you. Help you get settled in."

"Yes, *please.* I'd love that."

But Evangeline knew Cassie wouldn't come, because there was something Cassie wasn't telling her. And her closest friend in the world never would, more than likely, unless the universe conspired to make her.

"Ready or not, Evie. The rest of your life is imminent!"

Evangeline laughed. She threw a couple pointless hair bands in her suitcase and zipped it. "Hey, how's your dad?"

"Talking retirement," Cassie replied. "He'd been hoping for the detective job, but there's only one in our small town, who was *supposed* to retire and changed his mind. He doesn't want to hold out for it anymore, I guess. I understand." Something in Cassie's tone changed when she said, "He might even move out here. Or so he says."

"Hey, that would be wonderful! Right?"

"Of course. It gets lonely out here in Virginia, with only politicians, agents, and protestors to keep me warm at night."

They both laughed. Cassie had been celibate for years.

"If you don't make it to Switzerland in June, we'll see each other in the fall for our annual foundation meeting," Evangeline said. She lifted her suitcase from the bed and made her way through her apartment, switching off lights, yanking the cord when it got caught on something.

"Yeah. But I'll try to be there, Evie. I want to be there. For you. I really do hope you know how proud I am of you." Cassie's voice caught. "How much I love you."

"I love you too, Cass," Evangeline said, her worry growing rather than waning. She peered through the lace curtain. "My taxi is here. I'll call you when I get to New Orleans, so you know I made it safely."

She could almost hear Cassie smile through the phone. "You better."

CHAPTER 3
You

"Lisette, come on. It's just dinner. Maybe some drinks."

"I'm pregnant, Charles!"

Charles' cheeks flushed, some anger, some flustering. "I *know* that, of course, but I'm just trying to say it's no biggie. Just our friends. Casual."

"*Your* friends."

The comment was meant to diminish herself, but it cut Charles instead. Three daughters, and another one on the way, and Lisette still struggled to understand her position in the household. She'd given him everything... or at least, everything he could expect, under the circumstances. He'd give her the world, if only she'd let him.

But he understood now something he hadn't allowed himself to understand before. On some level, anyway, he knew Lisette didn't love him now and never had.

"You still love her?" Lisette asked. There was no jealousy in the question, only mocking accusation.

"No, and not for a long time," he answered, tired of reassuring her every single time Colin and Catherine came for a visit. "That ended when you began."

"Charming."

"The two things had nothing to do with one another."

Lisette laughed. "You love me because you can't love her."

Charles rubbed his hand across the week-long stubble lining his mouth and chin. "For the last time, I do not want to talk about Catherine Sullivan. Ever. Okay?"

"You never want to talk about anything. You only want to fuck."

Charles flushed again. She rarely spoke with such vulgarity, and contrary to how it had turned him on, years before, when Catherine had done it—*come fuck me, Charles*—it repulsed him coming from the sweet, young Lisette.

There was a problem somewhere in that feeling that he was afraid to identify.

"We ain't doing much of that with you about to burst," Charles murmured.

"You no suffer. I see you no deny yourself."

Charles whipped his head around. There was no way she could know about his afternoons in the Bourbon Orleans. "So that's a no on dinner, then?"

"Yes, Charles. That is no." She rubbed her swollen belly. "I play with Nathalie, Giselle, and Lucienne. Maybe, too, that son you no love."

Charles' eyes narrowed into tight slits. "Watch it, Lis. There's some things I won't tolerate. Even from you."

Time had softened the pain of Catherine's smile.

It used to take great effort for him to laugh at the jokes she'd make, or feign interest in her stories. To pretend everything was okay, when it was not okay, not even a little bit.

Gradually, he stopped thinking of the hazy swoon in her eyes as she sat astride him. He could hardly remember her big moony eyes when she'd ask, for the thousandth time, if he loved her.

Time, though, had also changed Charles.

With Catherine, he'd had love. With Lisette, he'd forced love.

And now, he understood, neither had been real, in their own ways.

Nothing was real anymore, except the love he had for his cherubic baby girls.

Nathalie, with her dark hair and wide, curious eyes.

Giselle, with bouncy blond curls and an interest in everything.

Lucienne, still a baby, but already so sweet and lovely.

And what would his Adrienne be like? He'd named her, of course, as he'd named the others, in the spirit of his French ancestors. He knew she'd be a little girl, just as he'd known the others would be. He no longer needed Lisette to love him, only to give him more of something to love.

Catherine was telling a story about her job as a transcriptionist. She was supposed to write down everything said, verbatim, and the doctor she worked for gave her some tapes earlier that week that were filled to the brim with expletives.

"I don't know if this patient had Tourette's or what!" she cried, laughing, wine glass dangling precariously. "But, oh my, I had to find another room because I was afraid that even through my headphones someone might hear!"

Colin laughed so hard he had tears in his eyes. Whatever problems in their marriage had led Catherine back to Charles for the last time, over four years ago, they were forgotten. His covert hand squeezes, his peripheral longing gazes… Colin was a man in love, again, and this time, with the woman she was, not the woman he hoped her to be.

Cordelia smiled tightly and sipped her own wine. "Lots of fucks, I take it."

"Every last one in the universe, I'm afraid," Catherine responded, grinning.

"Where's Lisette tonight?" Colin asked. "She's due soon, right?"

"July," Charles replied. "She's still nursing Lucie, so she's tired all the time."

"God, I remember that exhaustion," Catherine lamented. "Exhausting, but so worth it."

"I don't," Cordelia said with a bored look at her nails. "Nicolas had a wet nurse."

As was always the case when Cordelia decided to share something, the air was sucked from the room.

"Well, as long as a baby gets fed, what does it matter?" Colin chimed in, ever the diplomat. "And I don't think Carolina is nursing Cameron, either, isn't that right, darling?"

"He didn't take," Catherine said. "She tried pumping, but her milk production is low."

"Doctors say that's because of how hard it was, after Clancy. Robyn didn't breastfeed either," Colin said.

"Breastfeeding is such a riveting topic," Charles muttered.

"Only when you're not the one suckling the teet, eh, dear?"

Colin dabbed at his mouth and folded the napkin. "Anyhow, we best be hitting the dusty trail."

Catherine rolled her eyes, but was smiling. "You sound like your father."

Colin laughed. "We wouldn't want to leave Oz with Patrick and Isabella for too long. Might scare them off having their own little ones."

"You're still trying for another?" Cordelia asked.

A quick, dark look passed over Colin's face. "Trying, but the Lord hasn't seen fit to give us another. And if he doesn't, Oz is enough."

"I'll just use the ladies' room first," Catherine said, standing. On her way down the hall, she called back, "Oh! I nearly forgot. Cordelia, that book I borrowed is in my purse."

Cordelia grinned at Charles. "You can do the honors."

Charles groaned and pulled himself away from the table. He shuffled into the hall. He wouldn't have known Catherine's purse from the purse of the random woman at the supermarket, but she was their only guest, so he found the brown suede sack with ease.

He reached inside, rifling for the book, but instead his hand wrapped around a plastic case.

When he withdrew it, he turned it over, examining the light pink contraption. The clasp opened and he saw immediately what it was.

Birth control.

Charles looked up and locked eyes with a panicked Catherine.

"Please, don't tell him."

Charles dropped the pack back in her purse and thrust it at her. "We're well past the point in our lives where I'm compelled to keep, or care, about your secrets, Catherine."

Charles nearly fell asleep in the nursery room rocker, little toe-headed Lucie sleeping at his chest. Adrienne would sleep in here, too, when she was born in the summer. Giselle had only recently moved to her own suite of rooms, as Nathalie had the year before.

He was thinking about a new problem that had crept up, spreading its tendrils through the family. Or perhaps not so new, but only recently come to his attention.

This problem had a name: Soren LaViolette. And this problem had impregnated his sister. If Charles knew, everyone knew. Edouard, who wasn't in the business of touching his wife, certainly knew.

A swash of light fell across the carpet as the door opened. Charles looked up, prepared to be annoyed, but it was only Nicolas.

"Daddy?"

"Yes, son?"

"I can't sleep."

Charles rotated his wrist to check the time. Almost midnight already. He was surprised Lisette hadn't come in to chide him for not putting Lucienne to bed sooner. "Go downstairs and get a glass of milk, if you want."

"I don't want milk."

"What do you want, then?"

Nicolas dropped his eyes. "You."

A very familiar guilt crept into Charles, one specifically set aside for these moments with his son. He loved Nicolas. In his own way, he loved Nicolas twice as much as he could ever love his daughters. But his daughters were easy to love, and Nicolas reminded him of... of another time. Another Charles.

With some reluctance, he nestled Lucienne down into her bundle of blankets in the crib and followed his son out the door.

"Want me to read to you?"

Nicolas shook his head without turning around. He navigated the second set of stairs, to the third floor.

"Where are you going?"

"Can I sleep with you, Dad?"

And yet, it was times like this... when Nicolas needed him... that he was not so hard to love at all. Charles jogged up the steps until he was standing before his son. He lifted him into his arms and carried him up the last few steps, to the master's suite.

He could ponder the problem of Soren LaViolette another night.

"You bet, son."

CHAPTER 4

In Our Own Way

"Have you thought of a name?"

Soren rubbed her swollen feet, which were splayed out over his lap. Maureen rolled her head back against the cushion, miserable. She didn't remember being so *big* with Olivia. So unbelievably bloated and miserable.

That's how you know it's a boy, Irish Colleen said knowingly, but Maureen knew it was a boy because Colleen had laid hands on her and said so.

"I have," she said. "Edouard wants me to name him Alain."

Soren's hands stopped moving. "Edouard... what?"

Maureen sighed. "We've been over this. What else am I supposed to do? He could've turned me out on the street for this. The *one* thing I promised him was discretion, and now I'm pregnant?"

"To be fair, I managed not to get you pregnant for almost four years." Soren pouted. "I'm sorry, it's just hard for me to feel grateful to the man who gets to raise my son."

Maureen withdrew her feet, tucking them under her, despite her discomfort. "Soren, I love you, but that's not fair, and you know it."

"Nothing about loving you is fair." He sighed. "I know you

don't like to hear it. And I know you'd never leave him, Maureen. I'd never ask you to."

"Almost sounds like you're doing exactly that."

"I'm *not,*" he insisted. "Alain is my son, but Liv is his daughter, and she's happy there. Of course, I only know this from your stories, because you still won't let me meet her."

"You know why."

"Knowing why doesn't make it sting any less," Soren said. He hung his head. "I'm really not trying to make you feel bad, Maureen. I'm sorry. Some days are harder than others."

Maureen softened. She crawled across the couch and tumbled in his lap, curling her arms around his neck. "They're hard for me, too."

Soren pressed his lips gently to hers. His kisses were always soft, but demanding, as if a whisper of a promise he intended to keep but might never. The reminder that every kiss between them could be the last.

After that horrible day in Edouard's home office, her husband seemed to realize he'd gone too far. A week later, he'd come to Maureen and said as much, in his own way, and then pretended as if he'd never suggested they try things his way. He told her to continue on with Soren, in the same discreet manner, and they'd never speak of it again.

And they hadn't, for nearly four years. He reminded her, from time to time, that should she want another child she just needed to ask. Maureen *did* want another child. At one time in her life she'd wanted as many as her body could carry for her. But after that day in Edouard's office, her desire to rekindle anything with her husband, even for the transaction of impregnation, overcame her vision of motherhood.

And then she realized she was pregnant.

Her own relationship with Soren was complicated since that day. Her love for him grew, but there would always be a band of darkness between them. She'd never be able to completely wash away him reaching behind to coax Edouard to make love to him, too. She'd never forget his shame after, which was less about what he'd done and more about how far he'd let it go.

For his sake, for hers, she tried so hard to put that day behind her. If she could stay married to a man who had raped her, she could certainly go on loving the man who had tried to do something to improve that situation for her and ended up a victim himself.

They were forever locked in the limbo of that event, but it had also brought them closer. She was close to Soren in a way she could never be close with anyone else, man or woman, bound together by a secret so dark it simultaneously buoyed her love for Soren and ate her alive.

It had taken her nearly a month to work up the courage to tell Edouard about the baby. Her heartrate soared so high she saw spots and nearly fell out of her chair with the lightheaded feeling that followed. But Edouard only nodded, thinking. He said nothing that night.

But the next, he set his paper aside at dinner and said,

"In a way, you've made my job easier. Another child, and I didn't even have to come to your bed."

He said nothing else that night, and then the next, he said,

"I'll raise the child, of course. I know you've been forced to give one up before, and I wouldn't ask you to again."

How he knew that, she couldn't guess. She'd never told him that, or anything else so serious about her. They'd never had a conversation warranting such weighty topics.

Then, finally, the following night,

"You can have Soren until the child is born. After, I'm afraid, continuing on with him will only invite the very rumors we've been trying to avoid. The child will never know another father than me, and you'll never tell him or her about their real father. Letting him go will help with that. It might be tempting if he stayed around." Edouard frowned then and looked directly at her. "I don't suppose he'd believe the child was mine?"

"No," Maureen had said. "He knows better."

“Pity.” Edouard had returned, then, to reading his paper. The sports section, she thought, by the time on the clock above his head.

He said little else over the subsequent months, inquiring only occasionally about her doctor’s appointments or the health of her growing baby. But she had less than two months left until Alain was born, and that meant only two months left with the only man she’d ever loved.

Soren was different. He was a little mad, and a lot odd, and he had mood swings worse than Maureen. But he was hers, heart and soul. And she was his, God help her.

Soren pressed his lips to her belly, and she felt his tears tickle her skin.

God help her.

Maureen hooked her purse on the old hanger inside Blanchard House. It sagged with even the slightest weight, and she found herself doing the same.

She gripped the banister to stay the tears rushing, soundless, down her cheeks.

Edouard’s heavy steps sounded on the stairs. She swiped her palms across her face, sniffling the last of her sorrows away. He’d never liked an abundance of emotion, and she couldn’t bear his disapproval on top of everything else.

“You just came from Soren,” he said.

Maureen turned away to hide her reddened cheeks, nodding.

“I appreciate the sacrifice you’ll be making. I understand what it means to you,” he said, and she wondered why he was even talking to her. He only said words in her direction over dinner, and even then he was judicious.

And how could you understand? You, a man who has no time for love? A man who was forced to marry the woman he raped, and then did it again, in the name of that so-called love?

But he did understand love, in the way that mattered most to her. He was a wonderful father to Olivia. For her, he always had words. And he'd even found ways to give her his precious time.

"We can be a family," he said, and then she heard, but didn't see, his steps once again plodding back upstairs, toward his office, his safe place. "In our own way."

CHAPTER 5

Four Daughters

Irish Colleen set the kettle aside after pouring the steaming water into the saucers of her four daughters. When Elizabeth tried to take a sip, she shot her a scathing look. Three minutes. That was the rule.

"So, let me see if I understand this correctly. I have one daughter who, after over half a decade, is finally moving back to me. Another who, after slightly less time, is moving even *farther* away. And my youngest, my baby, is disappearing for the summer to Paris, of all places, and I risk losing her to the charms of that romantic city."

"I'm not going anywhere, Mama," Maureen said.

"No, darling." Irish Colleen patted her hand. "But you're not without worries. Will you ever tell your little one who his real father is?"

Maureen blanched. She withdrew her hand.

"Don't be cross with me, dear. I understand your marriage better than you think. I'm not judging you, but it does none of us any good to play make-believe."

"I wouldn't sleep with Edouard either," Elizabeth muttered, pursing her lips as she blew on her tea.

"You'll have all your grandbabies in one place for the first time," Colleen offered, shooting Maureen an apologetic glance.

"Think of it this way, Mama. You can come vacation in Switzerland," Evangeline said.

"I never visited you in Boston, or Colleen in Scotland, so what makes you think I'd drag these old bones on a plane to Switzerland?"

"I hear it's beautiful," Evangeline said with a shrug.

"And so is my home, Erin, but have I been back?"

Colleen smiled. This was Irish Colleen logic, and there was no besting it.

And when was the last time they'd done this? It seemed to Colleen there'd been many times when it had just been she and her mother, or there'd been one or more other siblings, but never only the sisters. She couldn't honestly remember the last time just the women had sat at a table together to talk.

Colleen was twenty-eight now. When Irish Colleen was twenty-eight, she had seven children to manage, her oldest already a decade into living. It was fun to compare, but hard to imagine the different directions their lives had taken. She tried to picture her diminutive mother and assuming father falling in love, but suspected the reason it was tough to conjure was because it had never happened. August had a broken heart, and Irish Colleen had the skills to nurse it. Quite the skills, as it turned out.

Irish Colleen pointed at the clock. They could drink now. "I think it's wonderful, Lizzy, that you and Connor are going to Paris for the summer. What a thoughtful gift from Augustus."

"Ana has changed him," Maureen said. "He's not the same man."

"He is," Colleen countered. "But he's regained some of the softness in him that he lost when Maddy died. You remember how he was with her."

"Never like that with any of us," Evangeline said.

"We didn't need it like she did," Elizabeth said. "Every Maddy in this world deserves an Augustus."

"Didn't save her, though," Maureen said, looking away.

"No," Irish Colleen said. She crossed herself. "Not even Augustus could do that, could he?"

Colleen raised her glass. "To Maddy."

Her mother and sisters joined her. "To Maddy."

"Are we going to talk about Charles, or is that off-limits?" Colleen asked.

Evangeline whistled through her teeth. Maureen and Elizabeth exchanged looks.

Irish Colleen spread her hands over the table. "I don't know what to say any more, girls. I truly don't. His situation has been volatile for a while now, and he adds to it as if he can't help himself. I don't think he can. Did you know he bought a petrol plant?"

The reactions from all four daughters were various exclamations of shock.

"Yes, well, he did. And a rice mill, too. Near Abbeville, I believe. He's been down there a lot, and don't ask me why. He never did have a mind for business, but now he's been talking as if he wants to buy up something in every industry. He mentioned last week he had need of a shrimping boat." Irish Colleen raised her hand. "Your hearing doesn't need adjusted. It's what I said. But he's a man of thirty now. I never had any illusions of control when he was a boy, and I don't now."

"Nicolas," Elizabeth said. "If Charles wants to mess up his own life, then that's his choice, but what about Nic? He might as well not exist. He's not letting Augustus and I kidnap him anymore. I even tried to say he should stay with us because his school is in New Orleans, but Charles has Richard drive the kid in, every single day, instead. What sense does that make?"

"None," Colleen said. "But Charles has always practiced his own brand of sense."

"I've tried too," Maureen said, shaking her head. "We have plenty of room at Blanchard House."

"I'll try when we get settled, too," Colleen said.

Elizabeth rolled her eyes. "Good luck."

"The girls, though? What about them?" Evangeline asked.

"You can't pry him away," Irish Colleen said. "He's only brought them to see me a handful of times. I have to drive to Ophélie to see them, and even then he acts like they're a hidden artifact at a museum."

"I wonder..." Colleen started.

They all looked at her, but she realized only she and her mother knew about the daughter that had been sent away, all those years ago.

"Charles obviously has his own reasons, and we'll never understand what those are."

Maureen turned to Elizabeth. "Are you excited for Paris?"

Elizabeth brightened, but dropped her face. "Yeah. I am."

"Paris!" Maureen said again. "If only..."

Irish Colleen smiled at her youngest. "I hope you come back married and happy, my dear. Truly, there could be no greater gift for your old mother."

"You're not so old, Mama," she replied, but they'd been saying this so long that it had started to become a lie.

Irish Colleen wasn't old, but she'd started to *seem* old. She no longer moved so fast. She took so many different medications she needed an organizer to stay on top of them. Her arthritic hands weren't always up for cooking, which hurt the most, because over meals was the one way they'd always connected. She'd even moved her bedroom downstairs, because climbing to the second floor was too hard on her.

And this, Colleen thought, more than anything else, was why she needed to come home. Because, for all their arguments and differences over the years, Colleen wouldn't have changed any of it. She wouldn't have wanted another mother, and she wanted her own babies to get this older, softened version of Colleen Brady Deschanel for as long as God gave them. She didn't want them to miss out on whatever good years she had left.

The matters of Charles, of Maureen and Soren, those weren't

hers to solve. She could be there for both of them, in whatever ways they allowed.

We'll sell the house, Mama. I'll move you into The Gardens. You can have your own wing. You never have to even see me, if you don't want, but when you do, I'll be there. Noah will be there. Amelia, Ben, and Ashley will be there.

Colleen caught her mother watching her over the table. She smiled. Colleen returned it. What went unsaid behind the gestures was bigger than both of them had words for.

Colleen had needed her mother more than she wanted to admit, over the years, and now, it was time to let her mother need her.

SUMMER 1980

NEW ORLEANS, LOUISIANA
VACHERIE, LOUISIANA
GENEVA, SWITZERLAND
WASHINGTON, D.C.
PARIS, FRANCE

CHAPTER 6
Dreams

They'd been playing a game in Paris. Connor, the mischievous game master, and she, Elizabeth, the eager participant.

Connor had embraced the planned elopement in exchange for latitude to perfect some mystery in the grand finale. He was a strategist, her fiancé, who had secretly, but enthusiastically, played games like Chainmail and Dungeons & Dragons with his boyhood friends, and saw every challenge as a carefully orchestrated series of moves. He promised Elizabeth he'd already made the arrangements for their "spontaneous" ceremony, but the catch was, she'd never know precisely when the moment was, until it was upon her.

Elizabeth had never been much for surprises, but after her initial fear of the unknown, she fell into playing alongside her love, even making comments like, *oh, the Eiffel Tower, this must be the moment! A cruise along the Seine? Come on, Connor, even a non-seer could see that coming!*

He loved her little predictions, and if the smile left his face for a moment in Paris, Elizabeth never saw. Instead, what she did witness was the Connor she loved, vacillating between boy and man; between a youthful curiosity that brightened her day, and a heavy seriousness in his love that made her stomach do flips.

But she loved these places more when he *didn't* drop to his knees with their rings. She adored the soft blurry evenings along the Seine, the Notre Dame holding court in rich gold lights. She was in awe of the ironwork of the massive Tour Eiffel, both standing at its base and atop the observation area, where she could see most of Paris, glittering and beckoning.

Elizabeth hadn't realized she had this in her at all, this romance. This love of things beyond her small world, which had sought to strangle her in all its inevitability.

All the bakeries were a wonder to her, with their delicious delights. Her favorite thing to do, from the apartment they were renting just off the Rue de Rivoli, was watch tourists read books in the Tuileries gardens, with their café au lait and croissants. After a week, Connor showed up with a couple of books he'd picked up in a small bookstore and said *they* were going to be the tourists reading, drinking, and partaking in the garden, and from that day forward, that was their morning tradition. Their welcome to the day.

After a few weeks, they settled into something resembling a normal life. Elizabeth picked up a little bit of French, enough to order her meals and ask for directions. Connor, who felt he had a responsibility to keep her entertained, tried to plan every day, but she gently assured him, between kisses, that it wasn't necessary. That they had all summer, and even the quiet moments, when it was only them and their thoughts, were a balm to Elizabeth's tortured soul.

For whatever reason, her visions were on pause in Paris. Not that she didn't already know what the future held... or at least the most salient points.

Elizabeth woke early that morning. Connor snored softly at her side, still exhausted from her rush of hormones the night before. Her desires came and went, and they were not concurrent with her love for him, which always grew, never waned. But when she craved his soft hands running across her own flesh, she craved them utterly. Totally. Until she was so blind with this desire that it was all she knew.

She settled into the small alcove she'd made into a window seat, nestling into the cushion as she eased the curtains aside. Down below, Paris was already alive. It was a city that rarely slept, passing between tourists and locals, back and forth. The palace of the Louvre caught the sun in her peripheral. It was one of the only things quiet at this hour. It was the most massive estate she'd ever seen, and a wonder to her senses. She wanted to go in and explore. Spend days there. Connor promised they would.

A man on the street below caught her eye. It wasn't that he was looking at her—which was odd enough, eyes locked on her from all those floors down, tinged with a strange intensity—but how out of place he seemed. Not just in the city, but in this time, this place, this... year. He had a shock of bright red hair that looked dyed, but she'd never seen any color like that from a bottle. A soft, jagged scar marked the side of his face, near his temple. But even stranger was that it appeared the man was carrying a... *sword.* A rather large one, from what she could see, sheathed in an aging leather scabbard, swinging from a thick belt that belonged in a museum.

But he did not. He was young... her age, maybe, even if his intense gaze belied a wisdom so ancient it confused the signals between her eyes and brain. The familiarity in the way he watched her was equally unsettling, as was the strange sensation that she *knew* this man. Perhaps had never met him, but knew him all the same.

No, not a man. Not human. Not like you, anyway.

Where did those words come from?

Elizabeth's breath caught, and she backed away, steadying herself.

When she returned to look for him, he was gone.

. . .

Connor unwrapped his sandwich. Elizabeth wasn't hungry. She was still thinking about that odd man on the sidewalk below their flat.

They sat along a grassy area at the banks of the Seine. There weren't many, but they'd found this one, a park it was called, though more of a judicious swath of greenery in a tiny enclave. Small enough most paid it no mind, but Connor liked to pretend it was their place. That only they could see it and enjoy it. It was their favorite lunch spot now.

"I was thinking we could check out the Louvre tonight," he said, after swallowing a mouthful of BLT on a baguette.

"Tonight? Won't it be closed?"

Connor grinned, flashing her a bashful look. "I'm on a research assignment for Deschanel Media Group. Signed off by Augustus and everything. Totally official."

"You didn't!"

He shrugged. "Will be nice to see all the cool stuff without crowds, don't you think?"

"I only wished I'd thought of it first. Nice move, Sullivan."

Connor flexed. His skinny arms didn't move the fabric much, but she liked him this way. Loved him in his beautiful simplicity and soft innocence. "Being awesome is my cross to bear."

"How long do we have?"

"From eight tonight until an hour before they open in the morning."

"Damn," she whispered. "Think we can stay awake that long?"

"I think we've faced bigger challenges." He crinkled the wrapper from his sandwich and shoved it in his backpack. "That's why we'll steal a nap first."

"But I'm not tired."

Connor crawled across the grass and pressed his lips to hers. "No, but you will be."

. . .

Elizabeth had walked past the large palace-turned-museum many times over the preceding weeks, but had never seen it so consumed by the loudness that came with the complete absence of sound. She heard every step her low heels made on the pavement, and there were no competing senses to drown out the thrumming of Connor's heartbeat as he pressed his palm to hers, fingers linked.

A woman met them at the entrance and went through the rules. She would leave them to their own devices, though there were hundreds of guards on duty. They had eight hours, to use as they pleased, but were not to stray from the paths designated for visitors. When they were ready to leave, they need only ask one of the lobby guards to unlock the doors for them.

Elizabeth felt a small thrill at being left virtually alone with some of the best art in the history of the world. Not really alone, of course, as a different guard nodded at them every few steps or so.

She marveled at the classic Hellenistic sculptures, spending extra time admiring Venus de Milo. She'd seen her in books, but nothing could prepare her for the impressive smoothness of the alabaster flesh; the utter love affair with detail. She lingered the longest amongst the art of the Italian Renaissance, which, to her, captured emotion in such a powerful and unique way. She especially loved Rafael's take on the Virgin Mary and John the Baptist. Then, she'd always loved art depicting the Madonna and Child, because there was no other love in the world that compared. It was the embodiment of what love should always be, and rarely was.

When they came to an especially interesting painting, Connor stopped to tie his shoes on a nearby bench. Elizabeth marveled at the interesting detail, of the soft, innocent features of Psyche, Cupid bent over her in protective love. François Gérard was the artist, and the piece was called *Cupid and Psyche.* Psyche was fresh and beautiful, all loveliness and innocence. But so was Cupid... that strange child of Venus who was meant to inspire love in others, but was, now, completely in love with the mortal Psyche.

"Elizabeth."

Connor's voice sounded so strange she couldn't help but turn.

He was no longer alone.

A guard flanked him, but the older man quickly peeled away his uniform to reveal a modest dress shirt and slacks. As he reached to adjust his shirt, she noticed the clerical collar underneath.

The priest smiled and waved. "Father Alan, at your service."

A dizzy lightness passed over Elizabeth.

"I told you I wanted to surprise you," Connor said, rising from the bench. "I know you were expecting something else. Maybe the Eiffel Tower."

"I..."

"But I really thought about it, Lizzy, and I thought, too, about all we'd been through. I thought about how, you know, like Cupid, at first I'd loved you by accident, but then only wanted to protect you from the world that brought you all this pain. I couldn't, of course, not really, but the more I tried, the more I loved you, until I realized, like Cupid, that to love you is to serve you, and to serve you is to love you." Connor stepped forward, lacing her hands in his. "Like Psyche, who represents the soul, and Cupid, who represents love, we are one and the same, Elizabeth. We always have been. And we will be, for as long as God sees fit to give us."

Tears streamed down Elizabeth's face, but she didn't dare close her eyes. She didn't dare miss even a single moment. "You did all this for me?"

"I had some help," Connor said, blushing. "Augustus really loves you, you know. Not as much as me, of course..." They both laughed. "But they all love you, Lizzy. Did you know I asked permission of every single one of your siblings before doing this?"

"What? Why?"

"I would've done it anyway," he said with a grin. "But I wanted them to know they didn't have to worry about you anymore. That I've got it from here."

Elizabeth wiped her cheeks with her palms. "I don't want you to worry about me, either."

Connor brushed her hands aside and cupped her damp cheeks. "I never worry, when you're with me. There's no safer place in all the world, for either of us, than together."

Elizabeth nodded and kissed him. "It's the only safe place for me."

"And me." Connor turned to Father Alan. "We're ready, Father."

Elizabeth repeated the vows with dutiful patience, but she knew later she'd never remember a single thing she'd said. Her eyes never left her husband's, as she passed her love, her trust, her entire self to him before the painting of Psyche and Cupid, which Connor had chosen, of all the thousands of pieces in the museum, to reflect the purity of what he felt for her. And it had always been as such with them, going back to when they'd only been the best of friends, tackling their schoolwork, and the world, with wide-eyed curiosity. As it had been when he followed her harebrained ideas about changing the future, and when she'd been so deep in her own pain she knew only one escape. As it had been when he made love to her, each and every single time. As it always was when he looked at her.

She didn't think of what she'd seen for them ahead. She thought only of the unspoken words passing between them as they linked their pasts to their future, sealing forever the bond that had saved them both, over and over and over.

CHAPTER 7

The Accident

Augustus closed his eyes, for the first time in his life believing that if he could only force himself to wake up then the day would prove to be a dream. That none of what he'd seen was real. That his Ana wouldn't be hooked up to machines keeping her alive. Keeping her breathing.

Irish Colleen's bony hand on his shoulder startled him back into the reality he wished he could escape. She squeezed and dropped into the chair next to him. Her heavy breaths were set to the steady beeping from the monitors. Kellan Jameson joined her, scooting his chair back toward the wall to give them privacy.

Augustus' mother didn't proffer false assurances, or deal in encouragement. All the healers he knew were gone, in this moment of his greatest need. Colleen was camping near Houma with her family. Evangeline, in Switzerland. Luther, overseas on a late honeymoon with his new wife. There were others, probably, but he didn't know who to call. Who to ask. Evangeline, who might have known, wasn't answering her phone, and the others had no access to one.

Charles was, at that moment, driving to Houma to try and find Colleen, but she hadn't said where she was going, exactly. She hadn't needed to. No one foresaw a day like this would come.

Maureen rested in a chair in the corner, eyes rimmed in red. Perhaps she was remembering a day, a decade ago, when another one of their beloveds had been in an accident involving a car. Perhaps remembering, also, how that had turned out.

A coffee appeared in front of him. He looked up. Cordelia.

He smiled. She smiled in return, a rather unnatural look for her but nonetheless kind, saying nothing as she settled into the opposite corner of Maureen.

It had all happened so fast. So much, so quick. The nurse popped in to say there were other guests in the waiting room, Sullivans, but Augustus didn't even know how they got to this moment, let alone how to exist in it. The room was already full, and none of the people who could help Ana were anywhere near her.

In a family full of healers, Ana's fate was left to the doctors, and one, as he left, whispered, "Pray."

But Augustus, who knew better, whispered, "Heal, Ana."

People liked to say that bad fortune came out of nowhere, but in the case of the car that had broken so many of the bones in little Anasofiya's body, it really had come out of nowhere, peeling out from the corner of Eighth just as the soccer ball went rolling into the street.

Every evening after work, this was their tradition. Ana would be waiting in the yard, ball in hand, babysitter laughing as she accepted her day's payment, and before Augustus could even take off his sport coat Ana was ready to go. The purple hues of twilight were a ways away yet, because Augustus was coming home on time now. For her. Because of her.

Earlier that day, he'd gotten word from Paris that his sister would now be signing her checks Elizabeth Sullivan, and he was in a good mood. The best in a while.

He chuckled and rolled up his sleeves, breaking into a low sprint when she started the game by kicking the ball before he even made it off the back porch. He nearly tripped trying to block her goal, throwing his entire body into it, no doubt ruining his shirt as he slid across the grass in what he thought was probably a pretty cool looking move.

The twinkle in Ana's eyes indicated it was, in fact, a pretty cool move. She looked at him as if seeing him for the first time. As if he was a superhero.

"Yeah, Dad! Cool!" she cried, pumping her little pale fist in the air as she leapt in admiration.

Augustus laughed as he futilely dusted the remains of the garden from his clothes. "Not cool enough, apparently. You still got one in!"

"I'll give you that one, Daddy," Ana replied, his little diplomat.

"That's very charitable, sweetheart."

She clapped her hands together, his incredible athletic prowess already apparently forgotten. "I'm ready!"

Augustus gave the ball a light kick, and it rolled, a little too neatly, right into her foot. She blinked indulgently, and then lifted the ball, backing up to return the serve to him.

Ana set the ball on the grass and ran back ten or so paces. With a sprint that made Augustus more than a little nervous for the impact coming, she reeled herself in and launched a kick so spectacular that the ball curved up and outward, sailing right over his head. Her eyes widened. His did the same. And then it disappeared behind a wall of foliage, beyond the yard.

Ana ran off after it, Augustus yelling at her to slow down, that he'd go get it. But his little determined princess either didn't hear, or didn't care, because she, too, disappeared beyond the safety of their subtropical kingdom.

Augustus heard the screech of tires. The impact. The screech again as that same car peeled off and away, leaving the broken body of Anasofiya Deschanel lying on the pavement.

The neighbor directly across from him on Eighth ran out just as Augustus dropped to his knees beside his daughter. There was already so much blood. Stars swam in his eyes, and the reality of the moment both hit him and slipped away, leaving him wavering between two threads of time. The woman ran back in her house, and when she returned, she had a phone pressed to her ear, tugging on the cord. She was screaming to get an ambulance, now, now *now!*

Augustus was afraid to check. Terrified that if he put his ear to her chest and heard nothing he would be swallowed whole by the understanding that the last thing he ever said to her was *no.*

But then she was pressed to his chest and he was carrying her, her little limbs falling in ways they should not, but she was *breathing.* She was alive, and he couldn't wait for the goddamn ambulance, he needed to save his daughter *now.*

Not like Ekatherina. Not like her. Nothing like her. He chanted these words with every step, which turned quickly to a sprint as he made it to his car, settling her gently into the passenger seat. It was all wrong, the way she slumped to the side, the way her arms folded. *No, you can't think of it now. Right now, you have something bigger to think about.*

The ambulance pulled in behind him as he raced to Touro, creating a break in the traffic to allow for him to speed through without hindrance. As he skidded to a stop in the emergency pull-out, the first responders were there before he could open her door, already working to save her life.

He ran behind her, catching glimpses of her bloody face on the gurney as they wheeled her into emergency.

It was an image he'd see burned in his nightmares for the rest of his life, no matter how this day turned out.

WE CAN'T YET KNOW THE EXTENT OF THE DAMAGE.

Tell me anyway.

Mr. Deschanel—

Tell me.

She has broken bones in every major part of her body. We can't know the exact number without causing her further harm. The internal bleeding has slowed since we went in and repaired her spleen, but she wasn't strong enough for us to stay in long. Even if she... even if she survives the night, she has a very long road ahead. The rest of her life will be impacted.

Not if. When.

Mr. Deschanel... Augustus... I don't want to give you false hopes. It won't help you, when the time comes, if the time comes, to make a difficult decision.

There will be no difficult decisions. Only a change in doctors if you can't handle her care.

Four hours. Four hours had passed, and the adrenaline had finally slowed. Augustus did everything he could not to replay the incident, because that would only send his anger into a pique that wouldn't help Ana. He needed as clear a head as he could find, if he was to save her.

Healers. There had to be others. But who could he ask?

He made a list of those he knew to be on the Collective Council. He was surprised to remember, given his disinterest in the whole thing. But his memory was his crown jewel.

Pansy.

Kitty.

~~Luther~~. On vacation.

Jasper.

~~Evangeline~~. Overseas.

~~Colleen~~. Camping.

Cassius.

He gave the list to Maureen. "Call the ones who aren't crossed out. They have to know. There has to be someone."

Maureen took the list and disappeared to do as asked.

· · ·

WHEN SHE WAS GONE, AUGUSTUS REMEMBERED something else.

It wasn't one thing, but several.

Ana, tripping over the upturned sidewalk outside their house, which had been pushed up by the knobby roots of the old oak holding court on the corner. He'd rushed to her side, but she had both hands on her knee, grimacing. When she pulled them away, there was nothing. No wound. No blood. No evidence.

Ana, accidently pressing her hand to a hot burner on the stove. Elizabeth ripped her hand away quickly, but not quickly enough. And yet, she'd had no burn where her hand connected with the heated metal.

Ana, falling off the swing set at City Park.

Ana, crashing into the side of the house after too many cartwheels.

Ana, getting pushed to the pavement by a bully at a class party.

Ana, who had, until today, never had a wound last more than a day.

Has she come into an ability yet? Colleen had asked, on her visit home over the winter.

Not that I can tell, he'd answered, though on some level had known it to be a lie. Perhaps he'd wished she might just be ordinary, at least in the way other kids were. That she wouldn't have to live with something that couldn't help but define her.

But he knew then.

And he knew now.

Denying it could kill her.

Accepting it might save her.

AUGUSTUS MOVED HIS CHAIR CLOSER TO HIS daughter. His reason for living. The sun in his dark world.

Was this his punishment, for believing he was ready to raise her alone? For daring to?

"Heal, Ana," he whispered in her ear, resting his head next to hers. "You know what to do. You've always known, and now you need to do what you did on the playground, and when you touched the stove. Do what you did when that kid pushed you. You need to do that, but more. A lot more." A sob caught in his throat and came out like a soft moan. If he cried now, it would be an acceptance of his lost hope. A harbinger of an end he would never accept.

Maureen watched him from across the room. Slowly, she rose from her chair and pulled it to the other side of Ana's bed. She rested her hand gently atop Ana's and said, "Heal, Ana. We're all here, darling, and we're ready to see your smile again. Heal."

Augustus' mouth parted, in an attempt at gratitude, but again only a desperate sound escaped. Maureen nodded at him. He nodded back.

"Heal," they said together. "Heal, Ana."

CHARLES ARRIVED WITH COLLEEN JUST AFTER THE witching hour. They came in the middle of the doctor squaring off with Augustus; the former, saying *I don't get it. It's not possible,* and the latter focusing to distract the doctor with some illusion or another.

Charles considered asking Augustus if he wanted the doctor knocked off permanently, but it didn't seem like the right time.

Colleen dropped to Ana's bedside and took her tiny hands into her palms. To others, it might look like she was praying, but she was doing exactly what she'd come to do.

"Come on now, Doctor, let the family rest a bit. You can pull out your microscope later," Maureen was saying, laying on the charm as she looped her arm around his, running her fingers over his white coat. She'd been a godsend to Augustus, in a way he could never repay. She'd spent hours making calls, and now there were other healers coming, too. All of them, probably.

. . .

IRISH COLLEEN DREW THE BLINDS.

"Heal, Ana," she said from the other side of the room.

"Heal, Ana," Augustus begged, though he knew now that she had. That she could. That she'd continue to, with their gentle encouragement. Somewhere in her slumber, she could hear their pleas.

"Heal, Ana," Kellan said.

"Heal, Ana," Charles said.

"Heal, Ana," Cordelia said, after a reluctant sigh.

"She's a very strong, very brave girl," Colleen whispered, pressing her lips to the fading bruise on Ana's cheek. "Very strong." She looked up. "Just like her daddy."

AT ONE, A NURSE POPPED INTO THE ROOM TO LET Charles know a call had come in from Vacherie. Lisette was in labor.

He looked up from the end of Ana's bed. "What? She's not due yet."

"It's what they said, Mr. Deschanel. And they said you better come fast. They've already called the doctor."

"Let's go," Cordelia said, when he didn't immediately move. She beckoned from the door. "You coming or what?"

He looked up.

"For heaven's sake, Charles, come on!"

Charles turned to Augustus, who nodded.

Ana would be okay. It was time for Charles to turn his attentions to his own daughter, soon to enter the world.

CHAPTER 8

Dust in the Wind

Charles flew through the oaken front door of Ophélie, pressing his body into the old slab with all the force he had in him.

"Adrienne!" he cried out, throwing his face north, toward the upstairs, the nursery, where his new daughter awaited him. "Daddy's home!"

Richard appeared at his side, reaching for his arm with tentative motions. Each time, he withdrew, looking in the same direction as Charles. "Charles, can we go sit in the parlor a moment? There's something we need to talk about."

Charles flashed him an uncommonly mean stare. "Now? Are you crazy?"

Richard looked away from him then, toward someone else, and that was when Charles noticed the doctor standing at the base of the stairway. His white coat was covered in swashes of blood, but Charles didn't immediately register this, or connect it to the moment.

Cordelia stepped forward. "You can talk to me."

The doctor looked down at his hands then up again. "Around—"

Charles cut him off by stepping forward, so close they could warm each other with their breaths. "Out of my way. I want to see my daughter."

Cordelia tugged on his arm. "Let's hear what the doctor has to say first."

Richard sighed from behind them, and in Charles' heightened state he almost thought it sounded like tears. But he didn't want to hear anyone's tears. He wanted to meet his daughter, and to have more, more... more! The sooner Lisette healed, the sooner they could plan for the next, and the next, and... "Get the fuck out of my way!" he cried.

Cordelia stepped away then, but Charles only had eyes for the doctor who blocked the path leading to his fourth, but not last, daughter. Lisette was yet young. She could have twenty, maybe thirty. With Lucie, she'd only needed a week to recover and was pregnant within a month of that!

But then Cordelia slid an arm gently through his. Gently. There was nothing delicate or gentle about his wife, but something in this very unusual gesture stayed his anger momentarily.

"Charles, darling, we need to listen to the doctor, and it might be best if we did it sitting down."

"I will not," Charles huffed, but he'd stopped winding further into his anger and now was merely in limbo, waiting. For what, he didn't know.

"Halfway through Lisette's delivery, she started bleeding. By the time we delivered Adrienne, it was evident we had a serious problem. I called down to the hospital in St. James, and also to University in New Orleans, but we couldn't even slow the bleeding long enough to buy her time to understand exactly where it was coming from and how to fix it." The doctor leaned into the banister and breathed out. "Lisette passed away twenty minutes after she brought Adrienne into the world. I'm very sorry, Mr. Deschanel."

Charles sidestepped all of them, laughing. His laughter carried across the room, bouncing between them as it increased in pitch and intensity. "Lisette? No. No, no, you're wrong. She's young and healthier than all of us. She's just tired, is all. Maybe she needs a year off or something."

Cordelia reached for him, but he dodged her, still shaking with laughter. "Charles—"

"She's not like *you,*" he hissed. "Not dead inside."

"Charles." Richard, this time.

"This isn't funny!" Charles screamed through his laughter. "It's not fucking funny, and if I find out whose idea it was to play a practical fucking joke on me, I'll fucking murder you!"

"I don't doubt that," Cordelia said softly. "But this isn't a joke. No one would ever find something like this funny. Come on, let's go sit down. We can take a few deep breaths and then we can talk to the doctor."

Charles stumbled away from her, from the weird and uncharacteristic behavior of the woman he'd been married to for seven years. It was like he'd never known her at all, with the soft, cloying way she looked at him now, as if he was a child in need of succor. But how, how could that be, when the woman had no maternal bone in her body?

How could that be?

Why wouldn't she stop looking at him like that? And Richard, with his hangdog defeated glances shared between Charles and the floor. The doctor, painted with exhausted defeat.

A shard of ice wedged itself inside the bloodstream of Charles Deschanel and he launched into life, knocking the doctor sideways as he flew up the stairs and ran, ran, ran, heading for the third floor, where Lisette had shared his bed for five years.

The door was closed. He wanted to kick it open, but that wasn't necessary, because it was unlocked.

On the bed was a lump covered in a white sheet.

It was a joke after all. It had to be. He'd *know* if Lisette was under there. If his sweet little French nymphet, who'd lived to please him, to love him, was lying lifeless beneath.

His anger boiled forth again. To hurt him like this... he'd have the doctor's license revoked so he could never practice again. He'd put Cordelia and Richard out on the streets with nothing, not a dime, to their names. Maybe he'd fucking throw them in the river, for good measure, to really show them what he was capable of when pushed to the brink.

Charles ripped at the sheet, letting it fall to a pile at his feet.

He stumbled back.

Lisette lay in a pool of dried blood. Her mouth, gaping open, set against a face as pale as the white sheet someone had laid over her. As if prepared to share something important. As if ready to call out Charles' name, one last time.

Lisette. Dead.

Charles leaped forward, spreading his body over hers as his hands reached for anything at all to beat, to destroy, as the world had destroyed his Lisette, and him. As everything he ever loved turned to dust and ash.

From the corner of his eye, he saw Cordelia sag in the doorway, face cast to the wooden floor at her feet.

COLLEEN ARRIVED AT OPHÉLIE LESS THAN AN HOUR after Cordelia called her. She didn't like to speed, but there were circumstances that required bending of laws, and this was one of them. The longer she left Cordelia alone to deal with Charles' dangerous grief, the more potential for disaster loomed. But it wasn't Cordelia who she worried most for, but the five children living under the same roof as a decaying corpse and a raving madman.

Cordelia held Adrienne to her chest when she answered the door. Colleen hardly had time to register the shock of wispy red hair atop Adrienne's baby scalp. Colleen accepted the bundle from Cordelia, marveling only for a moment at how Cordelia, when required, could step into the role of caregiver. She could've left the infant to sleep in her nursery, but she seemed to know that wasn't what was needed.

"There, there," Colleen whispered, pressing her lips to Adrienne's forehead. "Where is he?"

"He's locked himself in there with her," Cordelia said, voice raspy. Weary. "In the master's suite."

"She's still in there?"

"No one had time to even clean her up before we got home. She's still in her nightgown, still covered in blood," Cordelia replied. "And Charles... he, I don't know. Doesn't seem to notice. I don't think he's accepted reality."

"And the other children? Where are they?"

"Richard and Condoleezza are sitting with them in the nursery, but they're restless, Colleen. I don't think they should be here. They know something's wrong."

"No," Colleen agreed. She cast a look back over her shoulder. Maureen wasn't moving very fast as she waddled forward from the car. She was due any day now, and it had been a risk bringing her here to help, but the only alternative was Mama, and Colleen had come home to protect her, not expose her to war times. "Augustus will be here any moment."

"What should we do?"

"Charles can't stay here, either," Colleen said. "I can make the arrangements for Lisette, but not with him wrapped around her body. We need to get that whole suite cleaned up, and..." Colleen exhaled. She smiled gratefully at Maureen and passed their newborn niece to her. "Can you go to the nursery and check on the others? Maybe show them their new baby sister."

"On it," Maureen replied, moving slowly but deliberately toward the stairs. "Why, look at this beautiful girl, Leena!"

"She is lovely, isn't she?"

Maureen climbed the stairs, cooing at Adrienne.

"Augustus will take Nicolas and I'll take the girls," Colleen said, letting her planning give her strength. Control. "We'll take them for as long as is needed, so don't worry about that. They say Ana can leave the hospital tomorrow morning, and I'm sure it will be nice for her to have her cousin around." She put her hand on Cordelia's arm. The other woman looked down in surprise. "I know Nicolas is your son, but I think for the time being, it would be best if he stayed with Augustus. It would give him some normalcy."

Cordelia nodded, looking toward the stairs. Toward a scene Colleen couldn't even imagine, but that Cordelia would likely conjure the rest of her life. "I think that's best. For now," she said. "Besides, someone needs to stay with Charles."

Colleen almost sagged in relief. She'd been hoping Cordelia would take on that particular assignment, because someone needed to, and everyone else already had a role to play in the tragedy. "He has a room at the Bourbon Orleans."

"I know."

"He also has that flat in the Quarter, but at least at a hotel, you can get help quickly, if needed."

"You don't have to convince me. I was already thinking about it."

Colleen nodded. Where was Augustus? She felt terrible, pulling him from Ana's bedside, but Mama was there, and Ana would recover from her accident, soon, and with no lingering effects.

"Before your other brother gets here," Cordelia went on, seeming to choose her words with care. "Look, Charles is out of his mind right now. He's someone else entirely right now, and he's been saying some things... things that, if Augustus overheard, he might take to be true, when they're not."

Colleen frowned. "What do you mean?"

Cordelia looked again toward the stairs. "You have to remember, he's out of his mind. He's not thinking straight."

"Tell me."

"He's... well, he's saying that he killed Ekatherina and this is his punishment. That the universe has taken Lisette from him as retribution. An eye for an eye."

Colleen wanted to laugh. That's how absurd this sounded. And she would have, had it been anyone else saying the words.

Could it be true? It didn't seem like something Charles would do, not to an innocent young woman, but her brother had been on a slow but sure descent into madness for years. Perhaps he'd convinced himself she was evil. She'd no doubt broken Augustus' heart many times over, but....

"Like I said, he's out of his mind with grief," Cordelia was saying. "We both know better than to take that seriously, but Augustus might do well not to have to hear it, is all I'm saying."

This killed Colleen's suggestion of having Augustus take Charles to the hotel. Whether the words were true or not, they'd plant a thought in Augustus that would take root and never die. He would always wonder, and it would ruin whatever relationship existed between the brothers, forever.

"Are you okay to drive?" Colleen asked Cordelia.

She nodded.

"Good. I'll need you to take him to the hotel. Augustus will take Nicolas with him back to the hospital, and once I get the girls settled at The Gardens with Noah, I can come by the hotel and try to talk to him as well. I'll see to all the arrangements for Lisette myself, because he won't be in the frame of mind to do it. Do you have any information for Lisette's mother? If not, I know Mama will."

Cordelia nodded. "I can get it."

Gravel crunched outside as a car passed down the drive. Augustus had arrived.

"Good." Colleen this time followed her sister-in-law's gaze toward the stairs. "Can you help Maureen get bags packed for all the children? A diaper bag for Adrienne would also be a great help, but if you don't have things ready, I can get them in town as well."

"No. We do," Cordelia said, voice distant. "How will we get him out?"

Colleen smiled joylessly. "The locks on these skeleton keys aren't hard to pick. But I also have a brother who isn't afraid to kick down a door."

Cordelia nodded. Augustus stepped into the foyer, and both women went to their assigned tasks.

Augustus paused on the stairs, staying Colleen with a hand on her arm. "What happened, exactly?"

"The doctor is in the parlor writing it up, but it seems she bled to death during delivery. Had she been at a hospital, things might've ended differently. I don't know." Colleen exhaled and drew in a long, hard breath for strength. "Look, I think I've got Charles covered for now. Can you go help Maureen and Cordelia get the kids ready? I don't know how long they'll be with us, but I'd like to get them out of here as soon as we can. Charles is unpredictable when he's like this."

Augustus nodded. She hated to lie to him. She preferred him at her side, and even feared dealing with her brother alone. But if what Cordelia said was true, and Charles dared say it in front of Augustus... no, that was a disaster they *could* avoid. And they would.

"If I'm not out in twenty minutes, then come in," she said, thinking, but not saying, that if she couldn't convince her oldest brother to leave the room then her other brother was the only one equipped with the power to do exactly that. And, Charles confessing a dark sin or not, she might need additional assistance. "Oh, and don't call Colin just yet. Last thing we need is for Catherine to make a scene, thinking Huck needs her. You know?"

"Right," Augustus replied, giving her arm a quick squeezed before disappearing down the hall to the nursery.

Colleen turned toward the stairs leading to the third floor. She had no idea what she might find, but she had to be prepared for anything.

She tried knocking first, but hadn't expected that to work. "Huck, it's me. It's Leena," she called out, to no response. His sobs carried into the hall. She went to work on the door. As she'd told Cordelia, it wasn't hard to pick these old locks. Back when they were kids, they'd cut up some old wire coat hangers and placed them around different places so they couldn't lock each other out of rooms. Charles must have forgotten there was one on the frame above this door, too. Colleen felt for it and, relieved, pulled it down and went to work.

It only took a couple minutes before she heard the expected clicking sound. The door eased open.

Charles didn't look up, and Colleen wished she could divert her own eyes from the scene unfolding. Charles, tangled in bloody sheets, Lisette sitting lifeless upon his lap, her pale hair wound in tangles. As he shook, she swayed back and forth, no living muscles to guide her movements in a smoother pattern.

"Huck, we have to go now, darling."

"Fuck off."

"I called the Bourbon Orleans. Your room is done up and waiting for you."

"Go away."

"Brother." Colleen stepped inside. She wanted desperately to look away, but if she didn't immerse herself further into her brother's state of mind, she couldn't help him. "We need to get Lisette cleaned up. You know that. She deserves to be given respect in death. I can do this for you. I can take care of everything. I'm more than happy to."

"There's no respect in death," Charles hissed. He wrapped his hands in her snarled hair, rocking her on his lap. "This is what happens, Leena, when you try to save your family. You make the hard decisions... you do what others won't."

"You've always protected us," she conceded, afraid to tread the path he was leading them down. "I know that. We all do. But we're a family, and now it's time for us to protect you."

"You think you know, but you don't," Charles muttered through his incoherent sobs. "You don't know!"

"I don't need to know to help you."

"You don't know about Ekatherina! What I did, to protect Aggie from that miserable—"

Colleen silenced him with a hard slap to the face. He gaped at her, stunned from his reverie by complete shock.

"Don't you *ever* say that. Ever! And never in front of our brother. Especially if it's true." Colleen softened, reaching for his hands. She took one in hers. "She'll be with our people, Huck. I'll take care of everything. We'll put her with Dad. And Maddy."

"Dad and Maddy," Charles repeated in automated response.

"And all the others. All our beloveds," Colleen said, taking a careful seat on the edge of the bed.

Charles looked up, seeing her finally. "You don't know the things I've done."

"I know more than you think," Colleen said. "And it doesn't matter right now. What matters is taking care of sweet Lisette and those beautiful babies of yours."

"My babies."

"Nicolas and the girls will have everything they need while you grieve, Huck. Augustus, me, we'll care of them until you're ready again."

"I killed her, didn't I?"

Colleen shook her head. These words, small and innocent from her big brother, broke something within her. "No. You didn't do this. Childbirth is still dangerous for women, even with all our medical advancements. It's just a horrible accident, Charles, that's all. You didn't do this."

Charles' lips quivered. "You promise?"

"I promise." Colleen gently unwound him from Lisette. "Let me care for her now, Huck. You go into town for a few days, get some rest. We'll take care of everything. Me, and Maureen, and Augustus. You have a whole family who can take on the hard stuff. You won't have to worry about a single thing."

"Why?"

"Why what?"

"Why are you doing this?"

Colleen set Lisette back against the pillow and turned to her brother. "Because I love you, Charles. You're my big brother, and you're hurting right now, and I'm going to do everything I can do to make that better." Colleen wiped at her tears and pulled him to her chest. "I'll protect you now, the way you always protected us."

Charles curled into Colleen and sobbed.

An hour later, Colleen emerged from the third floor suite, Charles hunched over and leaning into her for support. When they reached the second floor, Augustus popped out of the nursery, but she shook her head at him. He and Maureen had their parts to play, but this next one belonged to Cordelia.

As soon as the house was empty, Colleen would make the arrangements for Lisette.

Colleen passed Charles to his wife at the bottom of the steps. He didn't argue as he folded against Cordelia like a lost child.

"If you need anything, Cordelia, call."

"I will. You'll come by the hotel? Later?"

"I'll call ahead first. If he's sleeping, it will be better to let him do that."

Cordelia nodded. "Thanks for coming."

Colleen smiled tightly, thinking of all that lay ahead. All that was changed, with a death of a young woman. "We're family."

Charles didn't remember anything following the moment Colleen guided him down the stairs at Ophélie. He had no recollection of the drive into New Orleans, or following their bags to the two-story suite, which wasn't his standing room, but Cordelia had apparently decided they needed more than that and went for a suite that was bigger than his flat only a mile or so away.

He didn't remember falling asleep, either, so when he woke, a wash of dusk spreading over his white comforter, for a moment he didn't know where he was.

Cordelia stepped out of the bathroom, toweling off her hair. "You're awake."

"What are we doing here?"

"You don't remember?" A look of panic flashed across her face, as if afraid she'd have to break the bad news to him all over again.

But he remembered. The last few hours were a blur, but the important details would demand space in his mind and heart for the rest of his days.

"Where's Adrienne?"

"With Colleen. She took all four girls. Nicolas is with Augustus and Ana, at Touro. For now."

"I see."

"That okay?"

"A bit late to be asking," Charles gruffed. But, for once, it wasn't Cordelia at the root of his suffering. To the contrary, here she was, though he couldn't guess why. He had a whole family who could've been talked into babysitting him. "It's fine. That's where they should be."

"She's beautiful," Cordelia offered. "Adrienne."

"Yeah? I wouldn't know." Charles ran his hands over his scruffy face.

"Red hair. Like Ana."

"Yeah?"

Cordelia's mouth pulled into a tight line. A smile, maybe. "Yeah."

Charles reached forward and tugged at the corner seam of her towel. She gave him a curious look, but nothing in it suggested it was unwelcome, so he pulled harder. The terry cloth slipped away from her and fell to the floor.

Cordelia was completely nude, standing before him. His wife. This should've been a sight he was all too familiar with, but, in all their marriage, he had never taken her complete measure. Her body was lean and lithe, with curves he hadn't detected through her modest clothing. Her cheeks flushed at the examination, but she made no move to reach for the towel.

Charles reached for her hand and pulled her forward. He didn't know what he wanted anymore. From her, from the world. Every action, even breathing, was powered by the moment, nothing beyond. He was too numb to consider where this could lead.

Cordelia surprised him further by climbing over his lap, straddling him as her arms looped around his neck.

"I don't know what's happening right now," Charles whispered, looking up at a woman who was beautiful to him in this moment, even if she'd never been before now.

"It's nothing." She kissed the corner of his mouth. Her bare bottom stirred something in him as she moved her skin across his exposed legs. "Or maybe it's everything."

"Or maybe it's nothing," Charles replied and moved in for a real kiss. He kissed her; his wife. A woman he'd never kissed before now, and might never again. "Or..." He angled her over the gap in his boxers, and waited, for the briefest of moments, for her to protest. When she didn't, he slid her over him, gasping at the softness enveloping him.

Cordelia didn't need the encouragement of his hands at her hips. She moved with slow but intentional strides as she rode him, at first gently, but then increasing in pace as his pleasure caused his eyes to roll back in his head. As she did... whatever it was they were doing, which Charles struggled to define once more because they'd never done it before now. Everything sexual he'd ever done with his wife had involved rules and strife, and he didn't know what it meant that he was lost to something real with her, for once.

Charles spilled long before he was ready, but she didn't punish him with a cutting remark or an end to their sexplay. Instead, she climbed over him and lay back against the bed, waiting for him to make the next move.

He thought he could love her then. It occurred to Charles

that he did love Cordelia, only in a way that was challenging to put to words. She'd kept his secrets, all of them. She'd take this loyalty to her grave.

Charles entered his wife once more. No timer. No rules. Just the two of them, finding their way through to the end of a trying day, and whatever lay beyond.

IT WAS CORDELIA WHO HELD HIS HAND AS THEY LAID Lisette to rest in the Deschanel family tomb at Lafayette No. 1.

Cordelia who promised him that, despite, the rain pouring down from the late summer sky, everything would be okay.

Cordelia who assured him they couldn't change what would be, only survive it.

Cordelia who cradled Adrienne to her chest when Charles dropped to his knees, hand on the tomb, as the priest led them in prayer.

Cordelia who promised him she would raise the girls as her own, and that he'd never have to worry about them having a mother.

On some level, Charles knew this couldn't last. Her careful understanding. His tolerance.

But for now, he chose to believe all of it.

CHAPTER 9

Goodbye Blue Sky

It was raining outside Evangeline's small, Spartan flat in Geneva. She had a chill, but it was too warm for heat, and besides, her space heater only worked half the time. Most of the Swiss she worked with proudly declared they needed no heat or air conditioning, and that Switzerland had such perfect, mild seasons that no one should. But Evangeline, who'd gone from the extreme, sweltering heat of subtropical New Orleans, to the harsh and unforgiving Boston winters, struggled to regulate her temperature in any climate anymore.

But the chill wasn't from the cold, but all the news from home.

Some was good. When she'd learned Elizabeth and Connor were married in Paris, she'd flown there for a quick weekend to congratulate and celebrate with them. She'd never seen Lizzy so radiant and lovely. So unrestrained in her happiness. Connor, too, was a new man, awash with the purpose found in being a husband.

The news from Ophélie dampened everyone's joy—except Elizabeth's, as they'd all made a pact not to tell her until she was home for the summer. There was nothing she could do anyway. Nothing any of them could do, though that didn't stop Evangeline from picking up the phone, more than once, to look at booking a flight back to New Orleans. It seemed unfair that Colleen, Maureen, and Augustus were left to deal with Charles' complete mental breakdown. Colleen assured her more hands wouldn't make lighter work in this case, but Evangeline's guilt ate at her nonetheless.

In truth, she didn't want to go home and deal with more family drama. Her work at the foremost nuclear research facility in the world had awakened something in her that had been there all along, waiting to be challenged. She'd flown through her schooling with ease, even at M.I.T., which was competitive for someone with her talents. But until stepping through the doors at CERN, Evangeline had never been in a room in which she was not the smartest, brightest, most capable. Working amongst the greatest minds in the world was humbling. It gave her something new to grasp onto, something bigger than herself.

And she'd met someone.

Evangeline tried those words out loud. She did it in front of a mirror, even. "I've met someone." She wondered if saying them would make them feel more real; validate her own confusion on the matter, or clarify it.

Over the years, as Evangeline allowed herself human connection again, she'd dated a handful of people she'd taken beyond the first date. Some men, some women. She liked them both and didn't know which she liked more. She supposed it didn't matter, because a spark was a spark. She'd always been attracted more to minds than bodies.

This time was different. He had a beautiful mind yes, but she loved how her hands felt tracing the hollow spots just below his belly, or his hard, sculpted shoulders. Loved his smile, which had always spoken to her, even when they were just colleagues.

She'd told Colleen about the others, but not him.

Evangeline went to turn the small heater on anyway, when the phone rang.

By the time she hung it up again, all the light had winked out of Evangeline's life. A gap in her world, once colored by confusion, filled in with a dark and terrible truth.

She picked up the phone once more, and this time she did book a flight.

To Washington, D.C.

"SORENNNNNNN!" MAUREEN HOWLED IN TANDEM WITH the push she gave after the doctor reminded her babies didn't deliver themselves.

Colleen held tight to one of her hands, while Irish Colleen mopped a cool washcloth against her brow.

"Careful what you say. Your husband might hear all the way down in the waiting room," Irish Colleen admonished.

"He knows this little asshole isn't his!" Maureen screamed, heaving short, tight breaths through her angst. "Hell's bells, Alain, come on already!"

Colleen glanced back at the door every few minutes or so. She had a fear Soren might show up, despite his assurances to Maureen that he understood what was expected of him once his son was born. But Soren had loved Maureen for half a decade now, and Colleen knew that was a switch not so easily turned off —for either of them. While she would've supported Maureen through any decision, even leaving Edouard for Soren, Maureen was committed to returning to her family and the promise Edouard had made to try harder, for all of them. A decision that could only be made by full commitment to the choice.

"Sweet mother of Jesus!" Maureen released at the top of her lungs, pitching forward as Irish Colleen rubbed her back, coaxing her to breathe.

"Not much longer," the doctor promised. "Just a few more big pushes, Maureen. You ready?"

Maureen threw her head back and screeched in response as she bared down.

. . .

Joseph Collins met Evangeline in the waiting room. She'd met him before, but he looked different. Older.

"She didn't tell me, either," he managed to say, pacing a tight line. "She never tells me anything, that silly kid." He shook his head, as if they were talking about her decision to cut her hair short. His hands shook. "I talked to the doctor, and, uh, he seemed to think she might not..." Joseph looked at the ceiling, closing his eyes against the glare of the harsh fluorescent lighting. "Well, that this might be her last night on earth, Evangeline."

Evangeline's knees turned to jelly. Joseph caught her before she fell, easing her into a nearby chair.

"I know it's hard to process. I'm not doing any better," Joseph said. He leaned into a pillar. "It's always been like Cassie to keep things to herself, but this time..."

"I know," Evangeline. She tried to look up. He was in shock, and needing her to say something to make it better, or easier, to accept. But there wasn't anything. Cassie's glioblastoma was incurable, and now, was taking her into the final stage of her life. Her peculiar behavior over the past months had an explanation, and it was worse than anyone could have ever feared.

But she had to pull herself together, because there was still time to heal her.

"Is she awake?"

"She comes in and out," Joseph replied, glancing around the room, searching for something. Bearings. Strength. This was one case he couldn't solve, and she saw every second that ticked by slowly killing him, too.

"Can I see her?"

"Of course. Yes. Yes, of course, come on."

He shuffled down the hall, past several rooms. When he came to hers, he let Evangeline go first and started to follow her, but then said, "I'll give you a few minutes with her alone."

She was grateful. She hadn't wanted to ask for such a precious gift, not when Cassie's minutes could now be measured in the smallest of doses, but she could focus better if alone.

Evangeline wasn't prepared for what awaited her in the private room. Cassie's beautiful golden hair was gone, replaced by a mess of thin regrowth; her full cheeks were gaunt and drawn, the color missing altogether.

Cassie was asleep, and as much as Evangeline had things she needed to say to her beloved friend, if her healing worked, then both she and Joseph would have as many minutes as they desired with Cassandra. That was all she could think about now, seeing her best friend whole and healthy again. Erasing the poison that had eaten away at her these past months while she suffered, stubbornly, alone.

Evangeline bowed her head and spread her arms over Cassie's thin frame. She inhaled, more a symbolic pull of strength than anything. And then she did something she'd done a hundred times before, though never on a scale of this magnitude. She healed.

Cassie's gravelly voice broke her concentration. "I know what you're trying to do, you crazy bitch."

Evangeline whipped her head up. "Cassie."

Cassie reached a weak hand forward and cupped Evangeline's cheeks. "I've always know what you can do, Evie. And it won't work on me."

Evangeline's tears ran quietly, unabated. "How the hell do you know what will work and won't work?"

"Because you and I both know about consent," Cassie said. Evangeline had to strain to hear her. "I'm tired, Evie. It's not only the cancer. I've been tired for a long time."

"Don't say that," Evangeline said. "You're still so young. There's nothing wrong with you that can't be fixed."

Cassie's blue lips curled into a smile. "Who said I'm broken?"

"I love you," Evangeline blurted. "I can't be in this world if you're not in it."

"And only half of what you just said is true."

"You have to let me try."

"You did try. What do you think woke me up?"

"You blocked it."

"I don't know if I did anything," Cassie said. "I only know it didn't work. And that it won't work if you try again."

"You're so sure, but you thought hiding this from me was a good idea."

"What would you have done, Evie? Come riding to my rescue? Put your own life on hold for something neither of us have any control over?" Cassie squeezed her hand with a weak grip. "I love you more than you'll ever know, and I am *so* proud of you. I am so, so unbelievably proud, like parents get, you know, when they think they had something to do with it?"

"You did," Evangeline said, wiping her tears. "I wouldn't be here if I hadn't met you."

"See, my life did have purpose."

"It's not funny."

Cassie kissed her hand. "I'm not laughing. Life is short, Evangeline. Shorter than we realize, sometimes. Don't be afraid to do the things and love the ones you love."

Evangeline bowed her head.

"Can you bring my father in?"

Evangeline started to fumble through agreement when she realized what Cassie was asking, and why.

"Do you want..."

"I want you here, too," Cassie said. Her breathing had slowed, with more spaces between the inhales and the exhales. It had started when she woke, but Evangeline only now realized it. "My two greatest loves."

An hour later, Cassie was gone, and Evangeline had never felt so irrevocably broken.

Colleen stopped by the bathroom on her way to the waiting room. She didn't have to go—she was still running on pure adrenaline—but she needed a moment to catch her breath. A splash of water on the face.

Since she'd moved home to New Orleans with her family, they'd lost a member and gained two. Three, if she counted her new brother-in-law, Connor. So much joy, mired in pain.

Colleen pulled in a deep inhale, straightened her spine, and went to go deliver the good news to her brother-in-law.

She found Edouard with Olivia leaning against him as he read a book to her. There wasn't much natural about the way he interacted with his daughter, but the smile on his face was real, and so was the attempt. Colleen had no warmth for the man who had married her sister, especially after the careless way he treated both Maureen and her soft heart. But Maureen believed his offer to do better was genuine, and Colleen had to believe that, too, if she wanted to envision her sister with the happiness she deserved.

"Edouard."

He looked up. Dark rings tinged the bottom of his eyes. "Is she okay?"

His choice of question was curious, but then, Lisette's unexpected loss was still so fresh for all of them. "Maureen? Of course she's fine." Colleen smiled. "She's resting. Mama and baby are *both* fine. You have a son. Alain was nine pounds, one ounce, and he has a whole head of hair."

"I have a brother?" Olivia asked, book forgotten. She leapt out of her chair.

"Yes, darling," Colleen said, kneeling down. She kissed her forehead. "A beautiful little brother for you to play with."

Edouard's eyes closed for a moment as he breathed out. "When can I see them?"

"Now," Colleen said. "Follow me."

Olivia skipped ahead, twirling in her yellow dress. Edouard lumbered at Colleen's side, awkward in his silence. She sensed he wanted to say something, and she almost broke the quiet to reduce her own discomfort.

Pausing outside the door, he found his words. "Things will be different, from now on."

"Sorry?"

"For your sister."

Colleen nodded, slowly. Who else had said those words, just yesterday?

Things will be different, Colleen.

Cordelia, everyone's emotions are a mess right now.

I don't know for how long. All I know is, right now, I can do this, for Charles. I can raise his girls. One day I'll resent them again, but we can all hope that day won't come soon, can't we?

I still think we should hire a nanny.

Loyalty is something Charles and I both know, Colleen. I know what you all think of me. You're not wrong. But I have never, ever been disloyal to your brother. You might say my hysterectomy was an act of disloyalty, but I gave him what he needed. A son. An heir. I owed him nothing more than that. And yet, I've kept his secrets. You and I both know what he's capable of. What he's done.

I have no idea—

You do. We don't need to discuss it here, or ever. I've kept his secrets. When the day comes, I'll find you, and we can get your nanny, Colleen.

The day will *come, though. Won't it?*

Cordelia hadn't answered.

EVANGELINE AND JOSEPH SPOKE TO THE CHAPLAIN IN A fog. He was a nice man, with a calming presence, but Evangeline's mind was elsewhere as she replayed every conversation she'd had with Cassie over the past year. Even with her consent, Evangeline knew Cassie had been beyond her help, but had she seen her a month ago? Two? Three? So much could've been different. Everything could've been different.

Joseph clutched tightly to the plastic bag that held Cassie's final belongings. Her Timex watch, a couple of rings, and the sundress she'd been wearing when she was taken in. Her sandals had been lost somewhere, they said. His mind was bare to Evangeline, because he didn't know any better, but she wanted to respect his privacy. Still, she picked up glimpses without trying.

How did the entire world change in forty-eight hours?

Evangeline slipped her hand through Joseph's. She told herself it was to give him strength, but she needed some too, from the only other person in the world who understood who Cassie was. What she meant.

"The Lord is my shepherd," the young chaplain began, and both followed suit, mumbling the words in dutiful repetition, minds equally numb and electric with questions. Hardly a day ago, Evangeline had been preparing for bed, calm and collected despite the chaos swirling around her family in New Orleans. Her life had been on a trajectory that scared and exhilarated her. The foundation growing beneath her feet no longer had sharp edges.

Everyone else Evangeline had loved and lost had died away from her. She hadn't been allowed to be there when her father passed, and Maddy lost her life in a car leaving New Orleans. Aunt Ophelia, too, died before they could get there to be with her.

There was something otherworldly about watching life slip from a person, and it was even more true when that person was someone you loved as much as Evangeline loved Cassie. Even as her breaths slowed, there was still a color in her, a sense of life beyond the flesh. A presence of spirit. But when Cassie's mouth froze forever in time with her last half-breath, that presence disappeared. Evangeline didn't know where souls went when they died, but she very much believed in the tangible nature of a soul. That it existed more soundly within a body, but existed nonetheless. She'd missed watching Cassie's soul depart, but she'd seen the moment it was no longer there, inhabiting her beautiful, tired vessel.

Somehow, that was the worst. Seeing the body of the woman

she'd told everything to, had spent hundreds of late nights talking with, rendered irrelevant.

A nurse knocked on the door. "I'm so sorry to interrupt, Chaplain. Mrs. Deschanel has a visitor."

Evangeline exchanged a startled look with Joseph. She started to turn, to get up, but the mystery was quickly solved.

Johannes Gehring stood in the doorway. His pale, Nordic cheeks were flushed with the fresh exertion of travel. He held a bouquet of flowers, which the nurse took and settled somewhere in the back of the chapel.

Evangeline tried to say something, but her speech failed her.

Her love was here. His beautiful soul had seen her greatest need and rose to meet it.

It was something Cassie would have done.

Johannes turned to Joseph. He reached forward and took both the man's hands in his. In his soft Swedish accent, he said, "I'm so sorry for your loss, Mr. Collins. Evangeline has always told me the most wonderful things about Cassandra."

"Thank you..." Joseph waited for the name.

"Johannes," he replied. "I work with Evangeline." He smiled and shook his head. "I love her."

Evangeline's chest ripped in half once more. Tears sprang to her eyes, blinding her. When Johannes folded her into his strong frame, she not only allowed it, she welcomed it, disappearing into the comfort and safety of someone else.

"Come, darling," he whispered and led her back to the pew, next to Joseph. "Let us pray some more for Cassie, and then we can do what is needed of us."

AFTER, THE THREE OF THEM SAT IN A PRIVATE ROOM TO discuss what came next.

None of them had any experience with this. When Joseph's wife had died, her mother had swooped in to make the arrangements. Evangeline had been too young to deal with any of the deaths that had come her way. Johannes still had both his parents, and all his siblings.

"Do you... do you have a place for her?" Evangeline asked. Her voice cracked under the pressure of the day. She drew a sip of water, and when she set it down, Johannes laid a steady hand over her shaking one.

"A place?"

"A family plot or anything?"

Joseph shook his head.

"Okay. That's okay." An idea jumped into Evangeline's head, and to her it was lovely and perfect, but she couldn't guess how Joseph might take it. "I have a family tomb in New Orleans. We have a few, actually, but the one I'm talking about is everyone in my immediate family and our ancestors. There's room... there's always room, with the way these are set up, which is interesting, really, but maybe not a topic for today." Evangeline tore at her wild hair. Why was she rambling? "Cassie was my sister. She has a place there, if you'd be comfortable with that."

Joseph looked off into the corner of the strange conference room, with wood paneled walls and matching tables and chairs. It seemed a good place to lose one's mind. "I would, Evangeline. That's very thoughtful. Thank you."

"And I'm taking care of the expenses," she said in a rush. "I won't take no on that. I know she didn't have life insurance, and she never let me help her when she was here, so I get to do it now, when she can't say no to me this time."

Joseph glanced up. He surprised her when he chuckled. "I might even have a mariachi band play. She'd just love that, wouldn't she?"

Evangeline returned the laugh. Cassie loved everyone and everything, but she had some strange exceptions, and mariachi music was among those things she couldn't abide. That, cheese on salads, and Ronald Reagan.

Imagining a Second Line down St. Charles with the band

playing mariachi instead of jazz gave Evangeline the first real joy since she'd landed in Washington.

"I'll make the calls," she said. "Where are you staying?"

Joseph gestured around. "I was staying here. In her room."

Evangeline shook her head. "I'll book you at the Four Seasons. With us." She turned to Johannes. "You have to get back?"

"No. I'm here as long as you'll have me."

"It might be a week or two. We need to get Cassie to New Orleans, and then the service, and—"

Johannes lifted her hand to his mouth. "As long as you'll have me. Tell me how I can help."

"When we go... it will be secret. I'm not planning to tell my family I'm there. I can't... not right now. Not on top of all of this."

"Okay."

"I want you to meet them, but not like this."

"Not amidst the chaos and the grief."

Evangeline nodded. "Yes."

"Whatever you need." Johannes looked at Joseph. "And you. I am at both of your service."

CHAPTER 10
Love Will Tear Us Apart

The remainder of Elizabeth's summer in Paris was underscored by a joy that left her wondering what evils lurked behind corners. These fears were the mortar holding the bricks of happiness together, and she tried her best to push them to their rightful place, but she couldn't live in her brick house without the mortar to hold it together. Her joy and fear coexisted in a symbiosis she wished wasn't necessary.

As their final day approached, the mortar seeped out from the cracks, coating the bricks. She'd managed not to think about their future at all, but without the magic of Paris to shield them from what lay ahead, it was *all* she could think about. It was everything. Their happiness now meant sorrow later. One wasn't possible without the other.

Their dinner that evening was one they'd enjoyed a dozen times before, at their favorite Italian restaurant. Connor liked to joke that the best food they'd eaten in Paris was anything *but* French, and he was right, but she saw Paris as a portal to the world and everything in it. The restaurant closed at midnight on Saturdays, and so they'd enjoyed first one, then two, and then a third bottle of wine, laughing and replaying their favorite memories from the perfect summer as evening turned into night.

When at last they stumbled out on the cobblestone, the clear sky was full of stars. Elizabeth threw her arms out and spun around, losing the pattern to a blur of space. Connor joined her until they both were dizzy, giggling, and falling over each other.

But even this joy caused her sorrow. The mortar, seeping out over the brick, coating it.

With every step, Elizabeth felt she pulled them closer to the inevitability of their destruction. Every delighted sound Connor made cast a dark pall over her heart, and she hated this, hated it! Why, why was she built this way? Why?

The Seine was quiet, or so it seemed. Connor stepped forward onto the bridge, to bring them to the right side of the river, but Elizabeth paused midway.

"Do you remember"—she closed her eyes, pushing a breath into the breeze that smelled of three kinds of wine—"when we tried to stop that steamship?"

Connor, giggling, stumbled back toward her, careening into the steel with a dramatic thump. "Mostly I remember us almost getting arrested."

"Stop. They weren't going to arrest us," Elizabeth said. "They were afraid for us."

"Well, yeah."

Elizabeth leaned forward over the railing. The light tide of the river below held just enough clip to carry anything away that might fall in. "I think I know now, why it didn't work."

"It didn't work because it can't work. We don't have that kind of power."

"We don't have power over things we have no power over."

Connor leaned his head back, taking in the stars once more. They were both so drunk, but there was courage in intoxication, and she was finding it now. "I just said that," he said.

"There are things we do have power over, Connor. Things we always have, we just never tried them."

"Lizzy, I think I might barf."

Elizabeth climbed up to the first rung, the bottom edge. She again leaned forward, testing her bravery. "I can't control what a steamship captain will do, or any of the people on that ship."

"No, really. Do you think if I barfed in the river they'd arrest me?"

"Doubtful. But I can control... what I'm saying is... I can control what I do. My own choices."

Lizzy wedged one of her feet into the carved fleur-de-lis pattern in the railing, raising herself higher.

Connor heaved over the side, oblivious to what she was doing.

She climbed higher, this time enough for her balance to wobble. "I know what I saw, for us. But if I jumped... if I went against what I saw and did something else, that would change the future. And no one could stop me, don't you see? A million things might have kept the captain on time for his departure, but nothing, no one, can stop me but me."

Connor wiped at the bile on his mouth and looked up, squinting against the lights. He blinked, not quite grasping. "Elizabeth, what are you doing up there? Get down."

"You're not listening."

"I am, I just really need some water."

"Connor, I'm being serious."

Connor sucked at the air around him, eyes glassy, as he tried his best to focus. "What are you saying?"

"I could change the future. Me. I can change what I know to be true." She climbed up so she was now balanced on the top of the railing. If she stood, she'd fall. She meant to fall, but not just yet.

"Stop it now." Connor's eyes flashed with heavy fear. He was suddenly sober. "Elizabeth, get *down* now, this isn't funny!" He reached for her, but when she wobbled, he leapt back in horror. "Elizabeth Jeanne!"

"I love you, Connor. There's nothing in the world more real to me than that love. Nothing." She glanced down at the dark, choppy water. "I don't want you to ever forget that."

A fresh gust tore her attention away from the river, and a

different horror crept up inside her as she saw Connor drunkenly climbing the railing.

"Stop," she said. "Get down before you hurt yourself!"

"But it's okay for you?" Connor wobbled as he pushed himself higher. His footing was unsure. Everything about him was unsteady. Elizabeth's stomach surged. "It's okay for you to throw it all away, but not me?"

"Get down!"

"I never thought I'd say these words, Lizzy, but if you jump, I jump."

"Okay, okay!" Elizabeth started back down, toward the safety of the sidewalk. Her heartbeat soared so high she was overcome with fresh dizziness. She stepped down, backing away. "See, I'm down. Now, you."

Connor went to do the same, but his sneaker caught in one of the curls of the fleur-de-lis. He struggled to break free but lost his balance in the jerk of movements. His foot came out of the shoe and his eyes landed on hers just before he went sailing, not toward the bridge but away, away from her, away from safety. She raced for the railing just in time to see him hit the water.

Elizabeth screamed as she watched her husband disappear into the abyss.

THEY GOT TWO ROOMS AT THE MONTELEONE. Evangeline felt foolish and a bit treacherous not staying with family, but she didn't have room in her heart to share her grief with others. She had Joseph and Johan, and that was enough.

Secretly, she'd paid off Joseph's house in Oregon. Evangeline recalled Cassie lamenting that he was on his third mortgage, partly to pay for her schooling, but also his own mounting medical debt. He wasn't the only Collins to have cancer, just the only one who'd survived. She paid those additional loans as well, and while she was at it, she took care of his credit cards. He'd be angry, no doubt, and nursing a bruised ego, but by the time he learned about it, she'd be back in Switzerland.

Earlier that day, they'd laid Cassie to rest in the same tomb where Evangeline's many ancestors spent their own eternities. She was relieved Joseph was okay with it, both because she felt in her heart Cassie belonged among the safety of the Deschanels and their ancient magic, but also because it meant she'd see Joseph again. He'd have to return, from time to time, to see after his only child, and that meant he wouldn't fade entirely away from Evangeline's life, either.

She lay awake that night, in their plush bed, listening to the French Quarter revelers. Johan's hand rested softly against her bare belly. She loved him, too, and she'd said as much, after collapsing in tears in her mourning dress when they'd made it safely back to the hotel.

She needed him. More, she wanted him.

But there was something else she needed as well.

Evangeline eased out of bed, lingering long enough to press her lips to Johan's. She shrugged on a sweater and jeans, left a brief note in case he woke and worried, and slipped from the room without stirring him.

She didn't know how far she intended to go, but it was a thirty-minute walk back to the Garden District. She aimed herself in that direction and willed her legs into action.

When she crossed Canal, that lively mix of cars, lights, and shopping, she felt a familiar presence behind her. She knew who it was before she turned.

Colleen greeted her with an enveloping bear hug, nearly sweeping her off her feet.

"I am so, so sorry about Cassie," she whispered as she kissed Evangeline's cheek.

Evangeline reluctantly pulled away. "How did you know?"

"Mama has coffee with Father Leonard every Tuesday. Remember?"

"Oh God. Mama knows I'm here?" Evangeline cursed under

her breath, though she wasn't angry, only annoyed at herself for not remembering there might be other ways her family could learn she was in town.

"No, I caught him on his way in. He asked how you were holding up."

"I'm alive."

"She was a big part of your life. It's okay to be sad."

"I hope no one cares. You know, that Cassie is with us now."

"Evie." Colleen kissed her on the lips. "No. She was as much a sister to you as any of us. And I won't tell anyone else you're here. I haven't."

"Thank you."

Colleen slipped her hand through the crook in Evangeline's elbow. "You wanted to walk, so let's walk."

"You sure? We could grab coffee or something. You don't have to walk with me."

"I want to, and I am," Colleen answered as they entered the crosswalk, passing over the neutral ground before landing at the edges of the Central Business District. "You're still liking Geneva, then?"

Evangeline nodded, shoving both hands deep in her jean pockets as Colleen leaned into her. "I like what I'm doing. It's challenging." Her breath unfurled in the late summer air. "And I've met someone."

Colleen missed a step. "You have?"

"I have."

"Well, tell me about him!"

"He works with me. He's tall... Swedish. From Gothenburg, but his mother is Norwegian. Like me, he was recruited straight from university, but he went to school in Zurich. A Cambridge undergrad, though, if you can believe it. He's smart, Leena... smarter than me, maybe. He comes from a big family, like us. He wants me to meet them at some family reunion he has to attend in the fall. In Malmö."

"Are you going?"

Evangeline nodded. "I think so."

"And when do we get to meet your handsome Swede?"

Evangeline thought of said handsome Swede, sleeping peacefully only a few blocks away. "I'll bring him home for Christmas, if we don't tire of each other first."

"I don't think you'd be talking about him if you thought it was a risk."

"No... I think... well, I think he's the one."

"That's a big statement."

"The biggest I can think of."

They crossed through the Central Business District and into Central City, passing a few blocks in silence. Evangeline was glad Colleen had found out and come. Glad to have the soothing relief her presence could bring. And now that she'd shared the secret of Johan, whatever grew between them felt more real and solid.

She'd bring him home for Christmas. She would. And if he didn't propose before then, well, she wasn't an old-fashioned girl, in any case. She'd do it herself.

"I love you, Evangeline," Colleen said as the old green streetcar rumbled past. "Be happy."

"I am," Evangeline replied. "I'm not so easily lost to my grief these days. I know how to come back now."

Colleen kissed her shoulder. "Good. I'm glad."

"Because of Cassie. Cassie showed me how to heal. Showed me why I should."

Colleen raised an imaginary glass to the sky. "For Cassie. A sister in all but name."

"For Cassie," Evangeline whispered through her tears.

Elizabeth struggled for breath as she paced the concrete bank of the river, her panic rising with every half-second that passed. It was so dark, like a sea of black and tiny pins of light, and she couldn't make out a single detail. Every light crest of water became a glimpse of her husband. Each time, a disappointment. She strained to see, screaming Connor's name, over and over until her voice was hoarse.

She couldn't swim well, but it wouldn't stop her from jumping in after him, if she could only *see* him. There wasn't anyone else around... no one else had seen him fall in, and so she was on her own unless she wanted to leave and find help, and there was no chance she'd give up an opportunity to spot and save him.

He couldn't be dead. She'd seen his future, and he still had to live long enough to see one of his own children die. And her. She hadn't died yet, so he still had to be alive!

You challenged fate, and this is your punishment. You changed the future, all right, Lizzy, just not the way you wanted.

Her horrified belief in the words of the unknown voice speaking these words to her on repetition grew to a near blinding terror, but then she spotted a flurry of movement from the corner of her eye, coming from a small picnic area closer to the stairs leading back up to city level.

A man, hovered over another man. The second man lying supine. Elizabeth raced over, one eye still fixed on the river, as she skipped sideways toward what seemed to be an important scene unfolding.

As she drew closer, the cold air beating havoc into her lungs, she turned her full focus to the two men. The one on the small patch of grass was Connor. The other...

She knew him.

Red hair. Strange clothes. Sword dangling at his side.

The man looked up. "I'm going to heal him. If I do not, he will die."

"We need to call an ambulance!"

"He will not make it," the man said, both hands pressed, palms spread, against Connor's wet chest. She needed to lean in, to look, but she couldn't. "I will heal him. In the same way your sisters heal when their own skills are required."

"They... what?" Elizabeth whipped her neck back to the

strange redheaded man. "Who are you? Where did you come from? Why are you here?"

"You may call me Tristan, but that is not my name," he replied. "As to your other questions, I cannot answer them, nor is an answer required, to save him. To right your wrong. To set you both back on fate's correct path."

"Look, I'm going to get help—"

But then he was in her mind. *Elizabeth. Stop. Let me do my work. Sit here, by his side. Hold his hand. Find purpose in another way. Let me do what you know I can do. What you have seen Colleen and Evangeline do.*

Elizabeth was stunned into submission. Until she felt the salty warmth trickle into the corners of her open mouth, she hadn't realized she was crying. She blinked, and the tears blinded her. She gasped for air. Nothing helped. Not her pacing, her unanswered questions. She didn't know who he was... she knew *nothing,* except that he was like her, in some way. Like the Deschanels, like her sisters, who could save Connor if they were here. And this man, who called himself Tristan, claimed he could save Connor and she had to believe that, because he was right. If they had to wait for help, Connor would be gone, and then, she, too, would be gone because there was no world worth living in without him.

She did as he suggested and settled down in the grass next to Connor, taking his hand in hers. It was cold... too cold. His flesh gave no response when she grasped it, and she felt no heartbeat through his palms, which always ran so hot. Was he too late? God, was he too—

Not too late. Now, be calm.

Elizabeth tried, but she couldn't help but replay her last foolish moments over in her head. She did this to him! She and her fears and her ego, thinking he'd be better off without her, without whatever years they yet had ahead of them.

Tristan turned to her, standing. He was quite a bit taller than he'd seemed crouching, or when she'd looked down upon him in the street. His red hair was bright even in the darkness, but it wasn't the red reflecting but shocks of silver woven through. The scar at his temple resembled a lightning bolt, but more crude, as if someone had taken a rusted, unsharpened knife to his face. His sword reached nearly to the ground, the sheathed tip swaying mere inches above the ground. He didn't belong in Paris, but she couldn't imagine a place where he did belong.

"He is resting. When we are done with our palaver, I will take him and place him in his bed. I've wiped his memory of the past hour. To remember it would destroy him."

"Tristan is my future son's name."

"Aye," Tristan said. "A decision born of this night."

"Why are you here?"

"I told you. To set you back to rights."

"Why?"

"You have seen your son's future. It must come to pass."

Elizabeth snickered. "So, you didn't come here to help Connor?"

"All life has value. Your son's has infinitely more than most."

"But why? I don't... I don't understand *any* of this." Elizabeth backed into the stone wall, still searching for solid breath. "I don't understand why you're here. Who you are. Why any of this matters."

"One day, you will."

"Why not now?"

"Because it is not determined that you should know this now."

"But you coming here and changing the future is?"

"I changed nothing. I was always meant to be here. To save him. To meet you and give you the name of your son."

"None of this makes any sense."

"No. But it will." He turned to Connor. "Shall we get him home? Restore him to a happier time?"

"He'll be okay? Really?"

"Aye." Tristan looked back at Elizabeth. "You cannot change the future, Elizabeth Sullivan. You can embrace it. You can live."

Elizabeth tried not to laugh. "Live. Right. Since you've seen today you must know what's coming for me later."

"Aye. A daughter will die. And then you. Connor's losses will be felt the deepest. But Tristan's will propel him into action. Action that saves everyone you love." He frowned. "Most everyone you love."

"You say to live," Elizabeth said, looking down at her husband. To see him like that, she would've thought him merely napping. She knew better. Would always know better, even if he wouldn't remember any of this. "But how can I? Knowing what's coming?"

Tristan considered this. "There may be, perhaps, a gift I can give you. Most would not consider it a gift."

"What?"

"If you were to know the precise number of days and hours left in your life, would it proffer the courage to live what's left of it?"

Elizabeth was taken aback. No seer had ever offered her this. She was certain Ophelia, at least, had seen her fate, but had never mentioned anything specific. And this man, whoever he was, *whatever* he was, was a seer. He'd seen this moment. He knew her eventual one.

Once she knew this, it would change her. She could never return to this moment and change her mind. She would always know, a countdown clock that never stopped and could never be reset.

But the unknown was what was killing her long before her time. She'd seen Danielle's name upon a tomb, but not an age. Not a year. What if she only had a few years left? But, then, what if she had a decade? Two? There was nothing in her visions suggesting Danielle died as a child, only a feeling.

She would die no matter what. The time, place, and means had been chosen, woven into the unbreakable fabric of time.

But she could make every minute until then count.

"Tell me," she answered.

Tristan approached her then. He smelled of honey and fresh bread. Of warm milk. He leaned in and whispered the answers to the riddle she'd been trying to solve for years.

Good on his word, Tristan told her the date, place, and means of her death. He even told her why.

"And lest you regret your acceptance of this gift, know that you were always meant to have these answers, Elizabeth. One day, this knowledge will give you strength. A strength that will be much needed as that final hour approaches."

Tears coursed down her cheeks. "Thank you," she whispered, though no words came out.

"Now you know what time is left. Only you can choose what to do with it."

"Will I... meet you again? Before the end?"

"No," he answered as he gathered Connor into his arms.

FALL 1980

NEW ORLEANS, LOUISIANA
VACHERIE, LOUISIANA
ABBEVILLE, LOUISIANA

CHAPTER 11

Just What I Needed

Life in New Orleans resumed at a languid pace. As summer faded to fall, the suspension of animation returning to the bustle of action, Connor wasn't the only one with big plans.

Elizabeth was so proud of her husband. In just a week, he'd be starting his studies as a law student, and within two to three years, joining the esteemed firm his ancestors built. He'd never wanted anything else, and, for someone like Elizabeth who'd never had a grasp on what she wanted at all, this was both fascinating and inspiring.

But now she did know what she wanted, and twice over.

She wanted to be his wife, and now she was.

And she wanted to help her family.

She'd come to this conclusion while they were still in Paris, moving through those lazy final days with soft contemplation. She'd probably never know who Tristan really was. In any case, she had to trust him when he said they'd never meet again, because he seemed to know everything else about her future. But his words and impact would linger. She wondered at this, at the strange way time passed for a seer, living both in the world they were in and in anticipation of the world they knew to be coming.

Other than Connor grieving her eventual loss, Elizabeth had seen almost nothing else about her future. She'd seen neither happiness nor sorrow. So was it so hard to believe Tristan when he suggested that, before she died, she *could* live? And she knew now… knew the *when*. It wasn't as long as she wanted, but it was, surprisingly, longer than she thought. It was enough to have a life, with experiences and memories. Joys and regrets.

You cannot change the future, Elizabeth Sullivan. You can embrace it. You can live.

But living involved purpose. Direction. She'd eventually become a mother, and while she didn't know exactly when that would be, she could guess, based on what she knew of her time left, and that guess put her first child, Danielle, at another year or two, depending. And there were other ways to live, than wife and mother.

Colleen sat across from her, sipping her coffee with the wide eyes of someone who regularly exchanged sleep for action. Her oldest sister never stopped going, not ever. A wife, mother, Magistrate of the Deschanel Magi Collective, and, now a PhD student, she never did anything halfway. Never had. And while Elizabeth guessed Colleen was wrong in the end about half the time, she never stopped trying to do better. Elizabeth supposed that was the best any of them could do.

Anyway, she could've done so much worse as far as big sisters went. Colleen was the only one she'd ever told about the future she'd seen for herself. Elizabeth hadn't foreseen this moment, where that information would become a function of her potential, but it only reinforced her belief in the fickle but finite existence of fate.

"I can't wait to hear all about Paris," Colleen said, smiling over her coffee cup. "That ring was his grandmother's?"

Elizabeth held her hand out, wiggling. "I love the modest band. You know I'm not much of a girl for glitters."

"You're not," Colleen agreed. "Connor asked us, you know."

"For your permission. He told me."

Colleen shook her head. "Yes, that, but it was more. He invited all of us to lunch and walked us through his plans. Very serious, he was. He asked for our opinions, and in some cases, help." She settled her cup in the saucer. "The Cupid and Psyche thing was his idea, he just didn't know how to make it happen. Augustus suggested the journalist pass, and, though Connor doesn't know this, he also made a phone call... you know, the kind only our bother can make."

Elizabeth grinned.

"Anyhow, Connor asked us about a ring for you. He intended to spend thousands on a diamond, because he wanted only the best for you, but it was Maureen who reminded him that a symbol of your bond would be more meaningful. And so he asked his brother, Thomas, if it would be okay if he took their grandmother's ring, since it was willed to both of them, you know, and Thomas apparently said he'd be a bachelor for life, so go for it."

Elizabeth flushed a deep pink, admiring again her simple gold band. Her siblings, they'd been right. No matter their differences, they were a family, and they were one, and they'd known exactly how to turn Connor's vision into a perfect reality.

"I think we might go back next summer. When he's on break."

Colleen brightened. "I think that would be lovely. And easier before you have children, for sure."

Two. Danielle and Tristan. "And your three? They liking New Orleans?"

"Amelia loves her Montessori. It was the same one Ana went to. She just started Monday, but she's already acting like she's the queen of the kingdom."

"It's a good one. I picked it out."

"So I hear. Ben is getting himself into trouble all the time, breaking dishes when he tries to move them across the room. I can't *wait* until it's *his* turn in Montessori." She shook her head, laughing. "Ashley is a sweet, quiet boy. He makes everything so easy."

"He and Amelia could be twins."

"I hear that a lot."

"I suppose I'll get to why I'm here," Elizabeth said. Her heart raced in anticipation. She'd envisioned this with all possible outcomes, but only one seemed most plausible, and it wasn't the one she wanted. Or needed. "I had a bit of an epiphany in Paris."

Colleen folded her hands and leaned in, listening. "Oh?"

"I don't know what I'll do with my life. You know, job wise." Elizabeth fidgeted. Her skin itched. The cool breeze suddenly felt clammy, invasive. "Maybe be a writer. Something I could do without being around too many people."

"You were always a good writer. A creative one."

"But I want something more than that." Elizabeth bowed her head, closing her eyes, before looking up again. "I want to be useful to someone other than myself."

"You were incredibly useful to Augustus for years! He couldn't have gotten through that period of his life without you."

"Yeah, I know. And you're right... with him, I was useful. But my whole life, I've been the one all of you have to look after. The one you felt the need to protect. You've shielded me from as much as you could, because I could never shield myself."

Colleen nodded, slowly, but said nothing.

"I know you'll have a Council seat coming open soon."

"You... what?" Colleen laughed. "You saw it. His retirement."

Elizabeth shrugged. "Yeah, I mean, this time no one's dying. That's good, right?"

"I suppose, but..."

"I want it."

"What?"

"The spot, Leena. I want you to consider me for it."

Colleen's focus broke. She pulled herself up straight, watching Lizzy with a curious, sideways look. "You want to be on the Council?"

"That's what I said."

"But why? Lizzy, you know this could be triggering for you."

"Probably will be," Elizabeth corrected. "That's okay. It really is."

"I still don't understand."

"Colleen, I'm not going to live as long as the rest of you."

"Elizabeth, stop!"

The threat of tears pulsed behind Elizabeth's eyes. "Can we not pretend? When it's just us? I told you, and only you, because I thought you'd understand and be able to speak rationally about it, when the time came."

Colleen's own eyes turned glassy. "I'll never be able to speak rationally about the loss of my baby sister."

"Fair enough, but it *will* happen. It'll happen before any of us are ready, but it *will* happen. Before that, I want to... no, I need to live. I need to find some purpose beyond Connor and the kids I'll have so little time with. I need to know I've done as much for my loved ones as they've done for me."

"Protecting you has never been a burden."

"Hasn't it, though?"

Colleen looked as if she'd been slapped. "It was better than seeing you suffer. I can't stand knowing there's nothing we can do to prevent you from seeing so many horrible things."

"Well, you can't. Ophelia was certain of that, and so am I. But you know what's worse, sometimes? This. The shocked looks when I suggest doing something that might, God forbid, trigger my ability. The wheels I can see churning inside your head, looking for yet another way to keep me safe." Elizabeth glanced at her iced tea, untouched, the condensation gathering in a thick layer on the glass. "I don't think it ever occurred to any of you that keeping me safe might involve letting me in."

"And if you're wrong? And it makes you worse?"

"I've seen my death, Colleen. It's not tomorrow."

"That's not funny."

"Did you know I'm twenty-two now?"

"Yes, Lizzy, I *know* you—"

"Did you know that means I'm old enough to decide things for myself?"

"You're no ordinary twenty-two-year-old, and you know it."

"When I die, I'll be no ordinary—" Elizabeth stopped herself. She couldn't reveal what Tristan had told her. Not to anyone. "I won't be ordinary, then, either. But I can be who I am and make it useful. When I see things, maybe I can use them to help. Maybe being around others who aren't afraid of their abilities will make me less afraid of mine."

Colleen checked her watch with a reluctant sigh. "I have to meet with my advisor."

"I'm serious about this."

Colleen met her eyes. "I know you are. And I need to think about it."

"That's all I ask."

Colleen dropped cash on the table and leaned in to kiss her sister. "I will, Elizabeth. Okay?"

Elizabeth nodded, biting back tears, as she watched her sister leave Brennan's.

Charles couldn't remember the man's first name. His last was easy. Fontaine. Like that hot broad from that movie his dad used to watch, *Suspicion.* Joan Fontaine.

He was a supervisor, or overseer, or foreman. Charles didn't fucking know. He didn't know fuck-all about rice mills, other than he was now the proud owner of three. This one, in Abbeville, was about two hours from home, the farthest away. But Colin always said that the business you keep away from you is the business that fails, so Charles decided this was the one he should spend time learning about.

Charles liked to say Vacherie was the bayou, and it was, but not like this place was. Folks in these parts were country folk in a way the uptown transplants from Vacherie only wished they were country folk. Lafourche Parish was small towns upon small towns. Hebert Rice Mill was one of several in the area, and was, Charles was told, also the biggest. He liked that. It's what sold him on the business. He wasn't used to being anything but the biggest.

The world around him was alive with sounds made by nature. He was used to most of them, but there was something altogether different about the soft echoes here. He was in God's country here, and although he wasn't here to worship anyone but his own damn self, he didn't shirk the almost constant reminders that there were bigger things in the world than his ego.

He'd never met the namesake, Hebert. Old man Hebert died, and the business went to auction, so Charles saw an opportunity.

Fontaine walked him through the tour, telling Charles in unusual animation about things called sorters and shellers, explaining a process he'd never in a million years find a need to know. All he cared about was the profitability, and that no one here had any mind to steal from him.

"My wife, Angelique, she's got lunch waiting for you," Fontaine was saying, and this caught Charles' attention. Lunch. He was *starving*. Just as quickly as he'd lit up, Charles frowned. He hoped it wasn't something fucking weird, like gator.

"We have a shift change coming up, and I need to make sure everything is in order." Fontaine looked guilty at this, but Charles really didn't give a shit about kernels and hulls anyway, so he forced a smile and told the man to go on about his business.

This was his twentieth or so tour in the past six weeks. Charles couldn't even remember all the businesses he'd bought up, adding to his growing portfolio. The day after Lisette's funeral, he'd marched into Sullivan & Associates and asked about profitable businesses in Louisiana, and they'd all looked at him like he'd sprouted four heads and started speaking Middle Persian.

There's a lot to learn.

I don't want to learn it. I want to hire people to learn it for me. I want to turn it into an empire.

After hours of discussion, both fruitful and not, Colin came around to what Charles was after. Perhaps he recognized the addict in him was in need of a healthier addiction, and there was nothing he could spend of the family's money that would put their wealth at risk. A few days later, Charles had a list of profitable mills, fisheries, and other local industries, and a restored sense of purpose.

He didn't think of Lisette at all after the day they put her in the cold cement of the family tomb.

And, though this wasn't intentional, he didn't think much of his daughters, either. Cordelia had it under control, she said, and though she'd been so weird these past weeks, he didn't think she was lying. She refused Colleen's offer of a nanny, which was even weirder given her stance on children, but he didn't know the first thing about kids, either, so who was he to judge? His dream of having a dozen daughters died with Lisette, but he could make new dreams. New empires.

Tiny pins of guilt nagged at him. He missed all five of his children. He needed them, more than they'd ever need him, he suspected. But a dark voice within him called from the abyss, telling him that the more he stayed away, the brighter their lives could be. Charles knew what his gifts to others were, and they fell nowhere on the nurturing spectrum. His love was violence. Passion. Two things that had no room in a child's life.

But he would build them an empire unlike any other. Unlike anything that had come before for the Deschanels. A foundation upon which they could build their own lives. That, he could do.

He found the small shack deep in the bayou, making several wrong turns along dirt roads before finally ambling down the right one. The approach was narrow and shallow, beset by encroaching knees from the nearby cypress. Spots of light peppered through the canopy of trees, dotting the path. A plume of smoke rose from a crooked chimney.

He wondered what Hebert had been paying Fontaine, for him to live like this.

Yet, there was something altogether inviting about the small, homely shack deep in the swamp. It beckoned him, filling his belly with a wave of welcome warmth.

The gumbo cooking on the hearth smelled incredible, but the woman tending it was what ensnared Charles' attention.

Angelique. Long golden hair swaying with her hips. Hardness painting her soft, sculpted features. Angelique.

He watched her over the bowl, letting her intense eyes eat away at his soul.

And when he finished eating, he asked, "Hey, I was thinking. Wanna fuck?"

Her green eyes sparkled in the dusty shack. "Jesse, my baby, that is, won't be awake for another couple of hours."

"And your husband?"

"Even longer."

CHARLES ROLLED HIS CAR BEHIND OPHÉLIE JUST AFTER midnight. His exhaustion kept him from parking it inside the old livery. He didn't even know if he could walk that far back to the house, with the afternoon he'd had.

Angelique. Dear Lord in heaven, he'd met his sexual match. Perhaps his sexual nemesis.

The woman had taken him to bed, but she hadn't been after what he'd been asking for. There'd been ropes and shocking violence. Whips. A thick-linked chain. He'd come twelve times. Twelve! Not even in the days where he pretended to go to college had he been able to summon such stamina. Every slap against his flesh sent his libido screaming into overdrive. When she did that thing with her finger... God, no one had ever dared try that on him before, but he'd let her, and if someone had told him that move was an instant orgasm he might've tried it on himself sooner.

In the morning, he'd be bruised, head to toe.

Charles smiled. Abbeville. Angelique.

He hadn't gone down for this, but it turned out to be just what he'd needed.

Cordelia was asleep in the parlor, Adrienne snoring against her shoulder. Charles hated to wake her, but knew Cordelia would want him to, so they could put sweet Ade back in her crib.

"Oh! I didn't mean to fall asleep."

"It's all right," Charles said, keeping his voice low. "Want me to take her up?"

Cordelia gently peeled the infant away. "Sure. If she wakes, she might be hungry. There's a bottle in the fridge in her room."

Charles nodded, as if he had a clue how to feed her.

But that wasn't true. He'd fed Nicolas. He'd done everything for his son, in what now seemed an entire eternity ago.

"Everything okay here?"

"Why wouldn't it be?"

Charles didn't know why he was forcing this small talk, but he thought it had something to do with trying to bring himself back down to reality after that surreal afternoon with Angelique Fontaine. "How are the girls? Nicolas?"

"The girls are fine. They had play dates with their cousins today, so they fell asleep hours ago. It's Tuesday, so Nicolas is in New Orleans."

"What do you mean?"

"We talked about this. He's living with Augustus on the weekdays now, at least during the school year. His school is only a mile from your brother's house."

Charles didn't remember this conversation at all, but it didn't mean it hadn't happened. He vaguely remembered saying no, unwinding this arrangement, but that had been months ago.

"Right. Okay, I'm going up to bed. You should do the same."

"I will. Oh, I almost forgot. Maureen called. She wants you to stand as godfather to Alain."

Charles was surprised by this. “Really? She said that?”

“She said that. The christening is next month, so you should let her know soon, one way or another.”

“Godfather,” he whispered as he carried his infant daughter up the stairs. After all the bad blood between him and Maureen, it was the last thing he expected.

And as he laid Adrienne down in her crib, holding his breath for the cries that would signal an even longer night, he remembered something else.

Other unfinished business, involving Maureen.

Charles decided he’d been remiss about this long enough. He’d deal with it before the christening, so Maureen could proceed with her new family in peace.

CHAPTER 12
Unfinished Business

With Connor giving his days to Tulane Law, Elizabeth needed something for her own. Colleen hadn't come back to her about the Council, but she couldn't wait around. Atticus was good company—though he seemed now to be more bonded to Augustus after spending the summer at Magnolia Grace—but sitting around a quiet apartment with a lazy dog wasn't helping Elizabeth's natural depression.

She tried sitting down to write, but found the only words she had were her truths, and she wasn't ready to commit those to paper. Not yet.

Augustus had mentioned Ana had a cold, and Elizabeth knew he didn't step foot in the office when Ana was under the weather. So she grabbed Atticus and jumped in the car, heading for her brother's.

She still had her own key. He hadn't asked for it back and probably never would. But she didn't live there anymore, and he wasn't expecting a guest, so she knocked.

Nicolas answered the door, but Augustus was hot on his heels, admonishing him, *what did I say about opening the door*?

"Oh, you *both* have colds?" Elizabeth asked, kneeling down to check her nephew's forehead. Atticus bounded past her, heading straight to Augustus for head pats.

Nicolas nodded. "Ana got me sick. I didn't get her sick. She's the sicko."

"I am not!" Ana howled from behind him before erupting in a coughing fit.

"I see," Elizabeth replied, winking at Augustus. He rolled his eyes, smiling. "Convenient that *neither* of you have to go to school."

"I don't know what that means," Nicolas said.

"It *means*—" Ana started, but Augustus told them both to get back in bed and rest.

They both huffed off, racing each other up the stairs before Augustus got on them once more, this time for exerting themselves when they were supposed to be resting so they could get better.

When they were gone, he hurled his body forward in a dramatic sigh. "They're more work when they're *not* feeling well."

"I can watch them. Go on into the office."

"It's fine. We just got the winter edition approved through editing, so this week is slower than usual." He pointed toward the kitchen. "Coffee? Tea? Apple juice?"

Elizabeth laughed. "I know where the drinks are, if I want one."

"I couldn't turn off my inner Mama if I wanted to."

"None of us could," she said, following him in. Atticus stayed at Augustus' heels. "Mama thinks I should take my estate entitlement and get a house for Connor and me."

"What do you think?"

"That the apartment is big enough for the three of us."

Augustus filled the kettle with water and turned the stove on. "You and Connor want kids?"

"I suppose so."

"Having a yard is nice, with little ones," he said. "Having

space for them to work off that insane amount of energy they never seem to run out of, is helpful."

"Plenty of parents live in apartments."

"True," he said. "I don't think you came by to talk about apartments and houses, though."

"Connor started his law program."

"I know. You must be so proud of him." He watched the kettle as if the intensity in his stare might speed the process. "We all are."

"I am. But, you know, I'm a little bored."

"I could bring you on as a part-timer, if you want."

"Thanks, but I don't."

"Figured, but you know the offer always stands."

"I know. Thanks." She stepped into the pantry to retrieve the tea for him. "How's Ana been? Not the cold... I mean from the accident. How's she recovering? I still can't believe you guys didn't call me."

Augustus pulled the teacups from the cupboard and nestled the bags inside. "And say what? There was nothing you could do from Paris, except worry. And..." He sighed. "I confirmed she can heal herself. I suspected it, but now I know. She's still new at it, so Colleen and some others came to help. She seems fully recovered, physically at least."

"But?"

At last the kettle sang, and Augustus quickly poured both cups, settling one in front of Elizabeth. He sat across from her. "She's been different ever since."

"Different how?"

Augustus played with his teabag. "She loved being outside. I couldn't even put my briefcase down before she'd have me by the hand, ready for a game of soccer. She always wanted to run and play. Now, she spends most of her time in her room. I thought Nicolas being here would help, but he's just as keen on hiding with her in the bedroom."

"What are they doing?"

"Reading. Brooding. I honestly don't know what four and five-year-olds do when they sequester themselves in their bedrooms."

Elizabeth considered this. "Is it fear, do you think? Because of what happened?"

"Maybe. I think that's part of it. I also think Ana has always been wired this way, and the accident pushed her further in that direction."

"Someone who prefers their own counsel isn't broken, you know. I've always sensed in her that she draws strength from solitude. Some just do."

"I know. But something broke inside her, Lizzy. I can see it. And I don't know how to fix it."

"Have you considered taking her to a counselor?"

"No, she's four."

Elizabeth sighed. "There are counselors for children, too, you know."

"What could she say that wouldn't make things worse? That she saved her own life, healing hundreds of broken bones with her mind?"

"Fair point, I suppose." Elizabeth fingered the rim of the cup. She'd been leading to this, but didn't quite know how to offer. "I could help. I could come look after her and Nicolas. I miss her, actually. I miss being her full-time auntie." *It would give me something meaningful to do. Some sense of purpose that I desperately, desperately need.*

Augustus placed both hands over hers. "Thank you, Elizabeth. For everything. From the bottom of my heart. But you have a family of your own to think of now, and it's time I consider a more permanent solution to this problem."

Augustus always looked forward to the weekly dinners with his mother. He started the tradition right after Ana was born; after Ekatherina died. It was time just for them, and as

Ana aged, he began to take her along, too. This time he brought Nicolas as well. They were both on the mend, and with energy to spare.

Sometimes they went out, other times they ate in. Now that Irish Colleen was living at The Gardens, in her own suite, they occasionally enjoyed a light dinner on the screened porch overlooking paradise.

Colleen took the kids for him so he could have the privacy needed for the conversation he intended to have with his mother. He hadn't told her anything, only that he needed some time alone with Mama. Colleen didn't question it. She took Ana and Nicolas by the hand and disappeared.

"You look very serious tonight, Augustus," his mother said. When they stayed in, he usually cooked, but tonight he'd brought her takeout from the English pub she sometimes frequented with Kellan. Augustus didn't know if Kellan and his mother were dating, but they definitely spent a lot of time together. He said nothing, because, with an empty nest now, his mother deserved happiness in whatever form she could find it.

"I suppose I am," he conceded. "I've been thinking a lot, and I wanted to get your opinion on something. Maybe your guidance."

She grinned. "You know I live for such rare moments."

He smiled back. "I come to you for advice."

Irish Colleen gripped his hand briefly. "Yes, you do. You're the only one who does anymore. How I love you for it." She sat back. "Ana seems to be recovering well."

"You know how she healed."

His mother nodded. "Of all the gifts of your father's people, that one might actually be a blessing."

"Not all of her is better, though." Augustus ran his hands over the shadow of hair on his chin. "And while I could blame it on the accident, I believe the issue is bigger than one thing."

"Go on."

"Ana has been very fortunate to have wonderful aunts and an

amazing grandmother. She's surrounded by love. But... there are times... I'm her father, Mama. I'm not her mother. And there are things I don't know how to help her with. Words I'll never know how to say. Lizzy keeps looking for reasons to come back and help, but the reason I sent her to Paris was so she'd live her own life. I can't keep relying on family to be surrogate mothers."

"Augustus," Irish Colleen said carefully, "I don't believe Ana is any worse off for not having a mother. Having said that, I understand and appreciate your meaning."

"You do?"

"I do."

"I'm not interested in love. I know what you're thinking."

"I daresay you don't."

He smiled. "I do, Mama. I know you want me to be happy. But I *am* happy. I have everything I could ever need in Ana, and DMG. I mean that, really. I don't need someone else to love. And I have no interest in dating. I haven't, since Ekatherina. I won't."

Nor do I have any desire for casual encounters, he didn't add, thinking about the incident at the DMV last month.

He'd been waiting almost thirty minutes when the pretty young woman sat next to him, finding the only empty seat in the sea of hot, cranky patrons fanning themselves with anything they could get their hands on. She chatted him up first, and while he wasn't in the talkative mood, he found himself engaging in light small talk, first lamenting the many numbers in front of theirs on the hand-pulled tickets, then exchanging facts about one another, some humorous, others bordering a lot closer to personal. She was a veterinary tech with a young son at home, about Ana's age. She was also a thrill seeker, something that piqued his interest, but he could not relate to at all.

An hour into their spirited discussion, she told him to follow her; she wanted to show him something. She disappeared down the dusty hall, toward the bathrooms and offices. He still had twenty or so numbers ahead of his, so he did as she asked, and as he passed by the crowd, entering the hall in search of which direction she'd gone, a hand snaked out, pulling him into a room. The bathroom. She locked the door behind him and then threw her arms around his neck and started kissing him.

Augustus didn't know why he kissed her back, but maybe the part of him that was turned on by the idea of thrill seeking peeked through, giving him a thrill of his own. He couldn't believe this was happening, but he wouldn't have the time or presence of mind to really dissect it until later. When she tugged at his pants, dropping them to his ankles, words made their way to his lips, but then died there as she pulled out his cock and placed it in her mouth.

He didn't last long at all, gripping the paper towel holders as his knees buckled. When she finished—swallowing... my God, he didn't need this like others did, but he was still a *man*—and noticed he was hard again, she backed herself up onto the sink and coaxed him forward, inside her, gently at first, and then... Augustus flushed even to think of the man who had taken his strange woman inside the DMV bathroom. It wasn't him, but it was, and it scared him to think he could lose himself so easily with the smallest enticement.

I've never done that before, he'd said.

Too bad. You're quite good at it.

She was out the bathroom door before he could respond, the transaction complete. He hid in there, ashamed, long after his number had been called.

And while sometimes, late at night, he still thought of that day, face flushed, libido aching, he was equally horrified that anything like that could ever happen to him again.

He'd never even learned her name.

He didn't want love, but he didn't want *that*, either.

"If I understand, you wish you had a woman in the house who could care for Ana, and perhaps see to the household, but without expectations."

Augustus laughed. "If only a woman like that existed," he said, but the hope of such a woman existing was exactly what brought him to this conversation with his mother. If anyone understood the practical side of love, it was a woman who'd married for exactly that. A woman who had never pushed him to be anything he wasn't. While his sisters all angled to set him up on blind dates, his mother did nothing of the sort.

"I believe women like that exist. Absolutely I do," Irish Colleen replied. "I even know of a woman who fits that bill."

Augustus gripped his hands in his lap, afraid to be too hopeful. "You do?"

"Do you remember my friend Annie Godfrey?"

"No. Not really."

"We sometimes play bridge together. Well, she has a daughter, closer to Maureen's age, but of course, still well into her twenties. Barbara. She was married, to a man she was in love with from the time she was quite young, fourteen or so, and he died of an aggressive cancer last year. Really very sad, poor thing. Chandler was her married name. Barbara Chandler. Very pretty young woman, but she's awful serious, like you. Annie was telling us a couple months ago how she wanted Barbara to go out and meet someone again, but that Barbara told her she'd never be interested in love again. She'd done that, she said, and didn't need it now. Her only regret was that she truly felt she was born to be a caretaker. A wife and mother. Annie told her men like that don't exist, that they come with certain expectations, but your old mama thought maybe she knew a man like that."

Augustus laughed. "All this time, and you *were* playing matchmaker for me."

"Not until you found your way to my dinner table, young man." Irish Colleen grinned. "Took you long enough. I was afraid some other brooding man approaching his thirties might come along and sweep ol' Barbie off her feet!"

His mother was making a joke, and she so seldom did it that it took Augustus a moment to catch up. "You're serious, though, about this Barbara?"

"I am. And, Augustus, I know you don't want more children."

"I won't change my mind."

"Barbara can't have children," Irish Colleen said with a soft sigh. "She found this out just before her husband passed. A double hit to her heart, poor dear. But... that also narrowed her choices in husbands, as you can imagine."

"Except for men who don't want more children."

"Yes, except men like that. Like you." She set her napkin over her food. "Would you like to meet her? Maybe have dinner, see if the two of you hit it off?"

"I don't need for us to hit it off."

"Augustus." Irish Colleen smiled patiently. "You want a wife, not a robot. You want a woman who will spark life and happiness with Ana. You want a roommate you can live with, with habits that align with your own. Practicality still comes with guidelines, you know."

"I suppose you're right."

"I'll talk to Annie straight away."

"This is weird, right? Feels more like a business transaction."

Irish Colleen laughed. "All my children are weird. I learn to embrace it, and all is well." She patted his knee. "No, Augustus. This isn't weird. It feels right, doesn't it? You'll have dinner with Miss Chandler, introduce her to Ana, discuss your mutual expectations, and, God willing, something useful to you both springs forth."

CHARLES GLANCED AT THE BLOOD-STAINED ADDRESS scribbled on a piece of paper sitting on the seat beside him. Before he'd showed up there, he was still delightfully dizzy from his day in Abbeville with the mysterious dominatrix whose husband ran his rice mill. But he had no choice but to break the spell. He couldn't delay this any longer.

Tears ran down his face, unchecked. He swiped crudely at

them, straining to see, blinded by both his own agony and the rain outside.

This was the last time. It had to be. They were all older now, each settled into the lives they'd chosen—except Maureen. She hadn't chosen this life, Charles had chosen it for her. And now, when she *was* choosing to invest in her unusual marriage and her family, he wanted to make that easier. He'd closed a door that still remained cracked, the light beckoning.

I did as she asked! I've stayed away! Soren pleaded, as Charles towered over him, knife at his throat. *Please! I don't wanna die, Charles!*

No, this was the last time. The last goddamn time.

This time when he wiped at his eyes, he was blinded by the blood he left behind.

Offing a LaViolette was a risk. This wasn't some middle-aged school teacher from the Sixth Ward. The LaViolettes were one of the only other families in New Orleans with as much money and influence as the Deschanels, and there was little chance that they'd leave the matter of a murder of one of their own alone. But it was too late to ponder that bullshit now. Soren was dead, and Charles had done it, and there was only forward, no going back.

You went too far this time, Huck. Way too far.

Catherine's voice.

She loved him. She let go, because she had to, but she loved this one. She didn't love the other guy, but she loved this one, and she'll know... she'll know, and will never forgive you.

"Fuck you, Cat."

You know what's worse? You didn't need to do it, did you? You didn't even have to kill him. Like he said, he was minding his own business. Doing exactly as Maureen asked.

"Fuck you!" Charles pounded the steering wheel with his bruised fist. Soren had fought, and fought hard, but Charles couldn't remember which bruises were from Angelique, and which were from his latest kill. Tomorrow would be even harder to distinguish them. "You don't know a fucking thing."

You're sick, Huck. You need help. I can understand why you killed the man who hurt Maureen when she was a girl, but this? He was a good man. He loved your sister. And Ekatherina? An innocent girl, sick from childbed?

"I'll always do what's best for my family. I don't need the understanding from some fucking ghost of the woman too scared to be with me." A horn sounded as he swerved into oncoming traffic.

No, then why is it me you're hearing these words from?

You didn't do this for Maureen, Huck.

"Stop it. Shut the fuck up!"

You did it for yourself.

For you.

Because you need it.

Because this, this, *is your true addiction.*

This is who you really are.

CHAPTER 13

Everything, Eventually

Evangeline stepped through the long marble corridor leading to the Council chambers. She'd walked this hall many times as a guest of her great-aunt, and over the past couple years, as a Council member. But she was now something else, too.

She was in love, and this time, there was no shoe waiting to drop. No secret double life—she knew this, she'd had Johannes investigated, though later told him the truth, and he didn't mind. He didn't mind because he knew her past, the way only Cassie had known her past.

But she was also grieving. She could love Johan better when he wasn't the link, the baton change from Cassie to him. She wanted to see him as separate of the purity Cassie's friendship had given her life, not the natural second phase. Cassie's death had hit Evangeline harder, in many ways, than Maddy's. Harder, even, than her father's. She'd been younger then, wrapped up in a different era of her life.

Evangeline didn't know how to tell Colleen she'd likely never move back to New Orleans. That, wherever her and Johan's life took them, it wouldn't be here. She'd visit as much as she needed. She took her family, and duties, with the seriousness deserved, but could be there for them, could live up to these duties, living elsewhere. She didn't worry about Mama anymore, with Colleen home.

Colleen stepped out of the chambers and lit up, surprised to see her. "You're early," she said as she folded Evangeline into her arms for a warm embrace. Her lips landed on her temple. "Oh, how I've missed you. How's Johannes?"

Evangeline grinned. "He's good. He's going to marry me."

"He... what? When did that happen?"

"I haven't asked yet, but I will."

Colleen shook her head. "How very Evie of you. What if he asks first?"

"He won't. I told him I wanted to."

Colleen laughed. "How *also* very Evie of you. When are you bringing him here?"

"Holidays. Until then, don't tell Mama."

"I won't, but she takes you being single as a personal failure, so you could always let her out of her misery..."

"Nah. Gotta save some presents for Christmas," Evangeline said and they both chuckled. But behind Colleen's laugh, behind her happiness for her sister was a deeper worry. Colleen had always tried to hide this, but was terrible at it, and Evangeline said so.

"I'm fine," she said. She kissed Evangeline's cheek. "Truly. I'm very blessed. I know that."

"But?"

"You'll keep asking until I tell you, won't you?"

Evangeline shrugged, but they both knew the answer.

"Well... I should have told you sooner, I suppose, but..." Colleen sighed. "I think Amelia may be an empath."

"And?"

"And?" Colleen repeated, incredulous. "You do remember the last empath in our family?"

Evangeline resisted the urge to roll her eyes. "Maddy was more than an empath, Leena. She was... she was a unique soul, you could say. She wasn't like anyone else, and being an empath was only the tip of the iceberg."

"Being an empath is what killed her!"

"Oh, come on, Colleen. Really? No. No, it wasn't what killed her." Evangeline reached out and took her sister's hand in hers. "It wasn't. What killed her was her big heart and, I don't know, her need to be at the center of the world's events. The stupid need to save things that can't be saved. I suppose being an empath fueled that, but that's who she would have been anyway."

"What if you're wrong?"

"When am I ever wrong?"

Colleen groaned and checked her imaginary watch. "How long do we have?"

"She'll be fine," Evangeline reassured her. "Not everything is a tragedy waiting to unfold, you know. Amelia has a mother who *knows* the warnings signs. Knows what to do. Mama did her best with us, but she wasn't even slightly equipped for the shit we inherited from Dad."

"Yeah..."

"She wasn't." Evangeline poked her sister's chest. "But *you* are. And you can train Amelia to protect herself in ways Maddy never could. You can teach her brothers to look for signs too. You don't have to do this alone."

"I suppose so."

"You're just afraid to be happy."

"I am not!"

Evangeline looped an arm around her waist, navigating them toward the Council chambers. "You are. Maybe we all are. But that's behind us, Leena. We got through the worst of it. Whatever's ahead are the best parts. Everything, eventually."

The quarterly Council meetings had been mostly perfunctory when Colleen took over as magistrate. In the past four and a half years, she'd focused on restoring purpose. On something other than reading over the past notes and making random observations. Luther's work building their network beyond their family had borne fruit, and next year they'd host their first get-together, at The Gardens, with allies from all over the world. Others like them.

She didn't know what Ophelia's eventual vision was, but she couldn't help but think she'd be proud of the work Colleen was doing.

But they had another topic for today. Cassius was officially announcing his retirement.

"I don't really have a compelling reason, other than I think it's time for new blood," he explained after the group hugs. "With my brother gone, and Eugenia focusing on family, I just think it's time for me to follow her lead, you know? I think it's time, is all." He looked at his son, Jasper. "Time for the Jaspers of the world, and the Luthers."

"Truly the end of an era," Pansy said, sniffling. "It feels like it should mean something."

"Maybe, maybe not," her sister, Kitty, said. "But things have changed. It feels so different now."

"Not bad, though," Evangeline jumped in.

"No," Kitty said quickly. "But different."

"Have you found my replacement yet?" Cassius asked. Though only officially announcing it tonight, he'd told Colleen weeks ago. "Tough shoes to fill, of course," he added with a playful flex.

"Elizabeth," Evangeline blurted. "Obviously."

"Why 'obviously?'" Pansy replied, smacking her gum.

"Obviously y'all's side has dominated the Council for way too many years and it's our turn," Evangeline retorted, doing her best impersonation of Pansy.

Pansy gaped at her, incredulous.

"It's not that simple," Colleen said tightly. "I'd love to see another Deschanel on the Council, but Lizzy's just not in the right frame of mind for this."

Evangeline spun on her. "And how do you figure that? Because she's a seer?"

"That's part of it."

"No, come on, Colleen. She's not a baby anymore. She's *married.* She's perfectly capable, and who else is there? We've already gone through Blanche's line, unless you wanna bring in the toddlers next?"

"I don't suppose you meant us," Jasper replied, pointing at Luther to his left.

"We already had to dip in the kiddie pool for you two," Evangeline said, eyes not leaving Colleen. Colleen didn't know what to do; Evangeline hadn't ever challenged her like this in a meeting. "Luther and his wife are having twins. I guess we could recruit one of them. Start 'em *real* young."

"What's gotten into you?" Colleen whispered, really wishing she could pull Evangeline aside without making the meeting even more awkward.

"I like Elizabeth as a choice," Luther said. "I would support that."

"I would get behind that," Jasper said.

"Elizabeth isn't up for a vote!" Colleen yelled, throwing herself back from the table. "Meeting adjourned!"

She was halfway up the stairs before Evangeline caught up to her. "What the fuck was that, Colleen?"

"Don't question me in a meeting, Evie! If you have something to say, say it after, but don't you ever—"

Evangeline pressed a hand to her sister's mouth. "Stop. Before you say something you can't take back." She slowly released her grip. "If you don't want Lizzy, fine, but you're really worked up about this. She's not a baby anymore. We can't treat her like one."

"You can act self-righteous about this because you don't know what I do."

"Then tell me, Colleen."

"I can't." Colleen reached for the banister, hands trembling.

"It's not my secret to tell. Even if it was... you don't want to know. Sometimes ignorance is bliss."

Evangeline backed away a step. "If you say so."

"She's not strong enough. She's not..." Colleen shook her head. She'd never been so tempted to tell anyone Lizzy's secret, but she couldn't betray the one thing Elizabeth had ever trusted her with... not when that one thing was the biggest thing. "She deserves a stress-free life, Evangeline. I won't play a part in seeing her hurt. We spent our whole lives watching her torment, and I want her new life with Connor to be the start of something beautiful."

"I understand," Evangeline said. "But isn't that Elizabeth's decision to make?"

"She won't have to," Colleen said, gripping the wood railing harder to stop the shakes. "Because I've made it for her."

AUGUSTUS SAT ACROSS FROM BARBARA CHANDLER AT Antoine's. While she ordered, he indulged a quick examination of the woman he might try to make his wife.

She was twenty-four, according to his mother, but looked younger, more like Lizzy's age. She had a soft, pretty face with dark hair falling around it in carefully styled waves. She wasn't as overtly pretty as Carolina, or as mysterious as Ekatherina, but was, unexpectedly, beautiful in ways that were more compelling, such as the quiet seriousness behind her green eyes. She had gone to an effort with herself for the dinner, but didn't seem nervous. Only anxious.

"I'm sorry about your husband," he said, after they ordered.

"I'm sorry about your wife," she answered.

"We're both too young to be having this conversation," Augustus offered. "But I've never found much use in wishing things were different."

"Regret is a wasted emotion," Barbara replied. Her pale hands gripped the flute of the wine glass, but she hadn't touched the

Chardonnay yet. "I believe in focusing on things within our control, not without."

Augustus smiled. "I suppose, you could say, that's why we're here tonight."

"You and I are both in search of something we think the other can offer."

"Can we, is the question?"

Barbara glanced around the room before turning back to him. "Whatever part of me was built for romance died with John. Maybe that's how you feel about..."

"Ekatherina."

"Ekatherina. My mother thinks I'll change my mind, but I won't. Not everyone recovers from everything."

"I understand. Not everything needs recovery."

"I thought you might," Barbara replied. "I didn't know, for a long time, what that meant for my future. I feel like I was born to be a wife, and mother, but now a critical piece of me is missing, and I can't imagine many men would be interested in what I have to offer."

"When Ekatherina died..." He'd never said these next words to anyone. "I don't think what I had with her was what you had with John. I didn't realize it at the time, but I do now. Unlike you, I'm not heartbroken anymore, I'm just... awake. I'm..."

"You know who you are now."

"Yes. I know who I am now."

"It doesn't matter how we got here. It matters that we are," Barbara said. "You have a little girl in need of a mother, and a household that would fare better with a woman's touch. I need a child to nurture and a home to make a hearth in, as they say." Then she surprised him by laughing. "As a businessman, you probably appreciate better than I do how this feels like a business transaction."

Augustus laughed after a pause, too. "I said something similar to my mother when she brought the idea to me. But I can appreciate the importance of a transaction that benefits both parties.

And Barbara… I can appreciate, too, that somehow there are two people in need of the same unorthodox things that managed to find their way to one another."

"Almost makes one believe in fate."

Augustus smiled. "Almost."

"Ana, right? Your daughter?"

"Yes, Ana. Anasofiya. She was named for her aunt," Augustus explained. "I call her both names, depending. Sometimes she seems more of an Ana to me, other times…"

"When can I meet her?"

"So you're… you're on board with this?"

"I think so. I think we get one another. We don't *know* one another, but we can fix that, over time."

"Tell me something, then," he said. "Something about you. Something you love."

Barbara pressed her lips together, looking toward the sky as she thought. "I love to read. I love the beach, especially Destin. I love needlework, though I'm not very good at it. And you, Augustus? What do you love?"

"My daughter and my company," he replied and put his hands up when she gave him an odd look. "I know, I'm not very interesting. I like to read, too, when I have time, but between Ana and work, I rarely have any left for a hobby. I never have much left of myself for anything, to be honest, which is why…"

"I understand," Barbara said. "I have no expectations of you, except kindness."

"I would never, ever…" Augustus trailed off. "You have no reason to ever fear anything like that from me. I don't know what I have to offer, but I do know I can give you kindness."

"And a little girl to love," Barbara said, smiling. "And so you know, while I don't have anything more substantial to offer, I'd be okay with you visiting my bed from time to time."

The unabashed way Barbara made this statement made Augustus's cheeks flush. He was sure she could see it. "I'd be okay with that, too."

Barbara laughed. “Is that a proposal?”

Augustus buried his grin in his wine. “I suppose it is.”

“So, something simple? Just our immediate family?”

“That would be my vote. We could have it at Magnolia Grace, or even The Gardens.”

“Either is fine. And a short engagement? Winter?”

“I’m a fan of the cold myself.”

“I’ll check my calendar and you check yours?”

“You should know, in full disclosure, I’m also raising my nephew for the time being. Nicolas. He’s Ana’s age. I don’t know how long he’ll be there.”

Barbara nodded. “If you’d told me you have twelve children running around, I’d be happy with that, too. Bring all your nieces and nephews over. We’ll make it a party.”

This was going so smoothly Augustus didn’t quite know what else there was to say. “Saturday would be a good day to come meet the kids. If you’re free?”

Barbara smiled and finally took a sip of her wine. “As it happens, I am.”

CHAPTER 14
Another One Bites the Dust

Charles dragged himself across the threshold of Ophélie, still drunk on the ministrations of his bayou mistress.

Augustus had said something to him the other day, when he dropped Nicolas off for the weekend. Something about how an addict will always find something to cling to. Charles, whose ego was still inflated by his miraculous ability to stay off the cocaine since Nicolas was born, didn't appreciate the comment at all, but he wondered if there was some truth to it.

Charles was at his worst when the world was still. He abhorred the quiet. He always said this was a byproduct of growing up with six siblings, but his upbringing was fortuitous, not the cause. He was at his best when swimming through the extremes of his life. With volatile women like Cat and violent ones like Angelique. With the other end of the spectrum, in the innocence of Lisette.

And was killing not also a drug? A dramatic swing of the pendulum, a high greater than any synthetic?

He'd asked Lisette to fill his house with laughter, and she'd obliged, but now he fled that same house, day after day, allowing his unpredictable wife to guide them through their formative period. It was easier not to question why Cordelia might be so amenable to the last thing on earth she'd ever wanted to do. Convenient for him to focus on his newest adventure into the extreme, the only one of his many whims holding his attention at present.

Did that mean Charles didn't love his daughters? He refused to believe that, but what other explanation validated his choice to be away from them so much? What other explanation justified his relief in Nicolas being with his uncle during the week now?

Cordelia asked him a question in this ballpark when she greeted him at the door.

"It's past dinner. You're coming home later and later."

Charles laughed. He threw his sport coat on the nearby armoire, and it fell against the bureau in a heap. "I didn't realize we were the type of family that enjoyed a nice dinner together."

"I don't care where you eat, Charles. Your girls do, though."

"They're too little to care."

"Oh? They ask about you all the time now. Especially Nat and Giselle. They draw pictures for you and ask me if you'd like them. They play house and one of them pretends to be you, and you know how they see you?"

"I suppose you're about to tell me."

"They see you as this distant figure that will only love them if they do tricks for him. And that's what they do, Charles. They put on some weird little talent show, one of them pretending to be you, and the winner gets a hug and a kiss. I'm no shrink, but I could probably figure out what that means. Don't you think?"

Charles' insides clenched in unison, fighting between anger and resentment. How dare she tell him this? She looked so smug, diagnosing their intensions, but maybe they played that way because they admired him? Loved him? Maybe his little girls knew how hard he worked to build their empire. Did Cordelia ever think of that? Of course she fucking didn't. All she thought about was herself.

He swallowed down the rock in his chest.

"Look. I'm not judging," she said, crossing her arms. "They're your kids, not mine. But I think we can both agree that I know you better than most people, if we can agree on nothing else. I know things about you I've *never* shared, and never will. I suppose in some ways we are actually well-matched." This made her laugh. "But you wanted these little girls so badly. Badly enough to write up that ridiculous legal agreement. Bad enough that you pretended to love Lisette so your own game of house wouldn't fall apart at the seams. So why the change?"

Charles didn't answer.

"What's going on in that demented head of yours, Charles?" The words cut, but her tone was even, unassuming. "What's happening with you?"

"As if you really want to know."

"I don't, necessarily," she agreed. "But you don't seem to have anyone else to talk to."

"I have Colin."

Cordelia snorted. "Colin doesn't know half the things I know about you. You can't take credit for that, either. He's either willfully ignorant or he truly is blind. I don't know which is worse."

She wasn't wrong. His entire friendship with Colin was predicated on this illusion. "He doesn't want to know. He never has."

"What are you doing, down there in the bayou? I know it's not work."

"I do plenty of work."

"Not at the rice mill you don't."

Charles laughed. She joined in. Cordelia was right, she was the only person who understood all the dark corners of his heart, and yet the last person he ever wanted to confide in. The mirror she held up showed more than cracks. It showed Charles for the person he was inside; the person hiding behind all the addictions meant to shore up the façade he'd spent his whole life constructing and fortifying.

"Fine. I'm fucking the foreman's wife. Happy?"

"You fucking anyone will never make the six o'clock news, Charles. But she must be something else, for you to set aside your daughters for her."

"I'm not—" Charles stopped. He was too exhausted to answer. It wasn't even the cuts and bruises anymore. His weariness ran soul deep, and the reminders of his failures only carved deeper ruts in the foundation. "Look. I don't want... I don't want them to... well, to *be* like me, all right?"

Cordelia's weird smile faded to a frown. A silence grew between them as she seemed to give this serious thought. "You think being around them, your depravity will just rub off? Like a bad scent?"

"How else do kids learn shit, if not from their parents?"

Cordelia laughed. "I don't think a whole lot of your skills as a human, but as a father, you've so far been a different man altogether. When you're around your daughters, you're, dare I say it, actually a decent person. You love them, and by some miracle of God, that love makes you different where they're concerned. Don't you get that the more you pull away from this, the more you pull away from your own humanity? Your own redemption?"

"Is that what this is to you? Watching over them? Your own redemption?"

"Oh, Charles," she said with a bemused sigh. "We both know my care of them has an expiration date. It always has. You just better hope it doesn't come before you figure yourself out, or then they'll really see a darker side of humanity."

THE FOUR OF THEM RAISED THEIR GLASSES TO A TOAST. *To children,* Noah said. *To friendship,* Rory added.

This was the first time Colleen and Noah had seen Rory and Carolina beyond in passing since they'd moved back to New Orleans. Carolina and Rory were back full-time now, with Rory working for the firm.

But they were now the parents of three children. After Robyn, Carolina got pregnant with their third child, a son. She and Rory had a falling out when he suggested an abortion, doing so out of a deep and justified fear for her life, but when Cameron was born without complications, they called him their miracle baby. After, Carolina didn't fight when Rory insisted they both take more permanent precautions to avoid future risk.

Cameron was a happy child, like his older brother, Clancy, who was now six. Cameron wasn't quite running yet, so he crawled after Clancy with impressive speed, following him everywhere. Robyn—who they called Ari—was content to play on her own now. She was almost four, with a full head of wavy golden hair, resembling someone whose name would never again come up at the table unless the topic was completely unrelated.

"And now Patrick and Isabella are finally joining the rest of us as parents!" Rory declared, refilling his wine glass. All six of their combined children played in the garden, just beyond the porch.

"Twins, would you believe?" Carolina added with a look that said, *oh dear me.*

"Luther and Josephine are having twins too," Colleen said. "A boy and a girl."

"Now *that's* trouble," Carolina said.

"Girls balance the boys," Rory said wisely. "Ari has such a calming influence on them both. Is Amelia like that, too?"

"A little. Ashley is our quiet one," Noah said. "They're all a bit introverted, I think. If any of them has the propensity to grow out of it, though, it's Ben. He's a natural showman, I think."

Carolina's eyes brightened. "Oh? How so?"

Colleen shot Noah a light look of warning. Although Colleen had once saved Carolina's life with healing, it was a strange sliver of the past no one liked to talk about. Anything inexplicable was unwelcome to a Sullivan, despite that she'd seen several of their brood work their own unusual magic from time to time. She'd often wondered if these similarities were what brought the families together, but also understood acknowledging them could be what tore the families apart. Rory and Carolina were safer and happier in a world where everything was just as it should be. They didn't want to hear about Benjamin juggling his toys in the air using only his curious mind.

"Oh, you know. Just likes an audience," Noah said, winking at Colleen.

"Ari doesn't seem to make many friends at preschool," Carolina lamented. "Sometimes I wonder if, you know, if she gets that from..."

Colleen placed a hand over Carolina's. "She doesn't. Amelia is like that, too. Some children just have different needs. Maybe we can set up some play dates between the girls?"

Carolina brightened. "Oh, I'd love that, Colleen. If it's not too much trouble."

"Of course it's not. Anasofiya is spending a lot of time in her room these days, so I'm sure Augustus will appreciate us bringing her along as well."

"Oh, yes! How lovely that would be, for all three girls!"

"All with first names beginning with A," Rory mused, to no one in particular.

"Until we invite Olivia," Noah teased.

The foursome finished off another bottle of wine before Rory insisted it was time to get the little ones off to bed. Colleen was a little drunk herself, a sensation she rarely allowed herself to indulge in. The languid pace of the evening, the hours of conversation with old friends, these things were a welcome addition to her chaotic life. She worried she might regret leaving Scotland, but her family was here. Her people were here. Her life was here.

They all exchanged hugs and kisses, along with promises to do this more often. And as Noah and Colleen watched their friends and their children leave, arms looped around one another, they drew strength from each other's peace.

They turned to leave as Rory's car pulled off, but Noah stopped. "Is that Colin? And Cat?"

Colleen followed his gaze, to where another familiar car appeared, from the opposite direction. She watched it pass down the one-way lanes on Jackson, pulling a U-turn at the light to park in front of The Gardens. "Yes... I think so." She checked the clock behind her. "It's nearly eleven. What do you think this is about?"

"I couldn't guess," he said, but jogged down the steps to meet them.

The couple exited the car. Colin, who normally went around to open Catherine's door, instead paced several steps ahead of her. Catherine lagged behind, arms wrapped around herself in clear discomfort.

"Oh good, you're up," Colin said and pushed past them both, without waiting for an invite, toward the door. Catherine followed, flashing an only slightly-guilty look.

Colleen looked at Noah. He shrugged. She sighed.

She closed the door behind all four of them, and before she could ask, Colin said:

"We need your help with something. Something unusual. Something, I think, only you can help with."

"Please," Catherine added, and Colleen didn't like the way the word sounded almost like begging.

"I'M PREGNANT."

Charles had just gotten his belt off when the words ripped through his skull.

"I'm sorry... I thought you said—"

"I did say. I'm pregnant," Angelique barked. She made no move to unwrap her robe. "It's yours."

"How can you be so damn sure?"

"I know who I am and am not sleeping with," she said. "My husband and I haven't shared a bed since before Jesse was born. Doubt we'll share one again."

Charles shook his head. "Okay, and?"

Angelique dropped her hands on the table. "What the hell do you mean, *and*?"

"And, are we gonna fuck or what?"

"Are you dense? Do you understand what I'm telling you?"

"You're pregnant," he said with a dismissive wave. "I'll pay to fix it. Doesn't have to ruin our day."

Angelique pulled her shoulders back. "You have some goddamn nerve, Charles. Some real goddamn nerve."

He laughed. "You can't intend to keep it."

"I can. And I do."

Charles' laughter ripped through the quiet, décor-less room. "You don't think your husband will notice a second little kid running around, that's not his?"

"No," Angelique said, never missing a beat. "I don't think he'll notice anything because I intend to divorce him. Just as you'll divorce your wife."

"That's not what this is."

"It might not have been before, but it is now."

"Are you crazy, woman?"

"Are you?"

Charles re-buckled his belt. He searched for his sport coat. It was incredible to him how fast he could fall out of lust, but he had. Whatever welcome insanity she'd brought to his life was now poison. She was poison. This rickety shack in the bayou was poison.

"I guess we're done here."

"Oh, no." Angelique stormed across the room, robe flying. She was suddenly no longer pretty, but homely, like a pigeon. "You don't get to walk away from this."

"Oh yeah? Watch me." Charles reached for the door.

"I'll tell him. I'll tell my husband, and then I'll put out a goddamn ad in every paper in the state."

"What do I care?" Charles retorted, but she had his attention. An affair was one thing... a child was another.

"You'll care when my husband can't control his rage. When he shows up to your beautiful home in Vacherie and looks in on your sweet, little—"

Charles didn't remember putting his hands at her neck. He didn't even remember crossing the room. Angelique clawed at his knuckles, scratching for breath. "You fucking dare come near my family and I'll feed your son to the fucking gators, and not a damn person in this state, in this country, in this *world* will do shit about it. Not one, Angelique. Don't think I'm serious? That's further proof that you don't know me at all. That you don't know my history... what I'm capable of. But because I'm not a completely uncharitable monster, you'll start getting monthly checks, enough money to change your life for the better, if you want it to. It's your choice. But make no fucking mistake, woman, if you come after anyone bearing my blood, it will be the last thing you or anyone bearing yours ever does."

Charles was shaking when he started the car.

He knew the checks wouldn't be enough. Angelique's pride was bigger than her greed.

Fontaine. The nameless husband.

Soren was supposed to be the last.

Yes, he was. But as long as the husband still walked the earth, providing for Angelique and her little brat, she'd still have a lifeline.

Charles had no choice but to sever it.

"THIS WHOLE THING IS HONESTLY SO STRANGE," Catherine said, pacing the parlor in her slippers. Neither she nor Colin had bothered to change into regular clothes before coming over, something Colleen noted with a sinking fear.

"I didn't believe it at first," Colin said.

"Oh, I still don't know if I do!" Catherine said, with a hollow laugh.

"There's no other explanation, though, is there? If it's happening to both of us?"

"You're the one who compared it to whatever the Deschanels can do, not me!"

"I have no other frame of reference, dear!"

"Doesn't make it true, dear!"

"And how else would you explain an otherwise unremarkable couple having a shared hallucination? Huh?"

Colleen put her hands out. "Hey, now. It's okay. Why don't you both sit down and start from the beginning."

"I'll grab some water," Noah offered, disappearing. She hoped he returned soon. She suspected she'd need him for whatever was about to happen.

Colin reached for his wife, but she ripped her robe away and sat down in a single chair, across from where he reluctantly sank into the loveseat.

"Something strange is happening with Oz," Colin began.

"Nothing is wrong with our son!" Catherine screamed.

"Cat, please. The children are in bed," Colleen said, though there was little risk of her histrionics carrying across the estate. But she didn't want to hear it, either. When Catherine worked herself up like this, there was no telling where she might take herself.

"Mine should be, too, but no!"

"Catherine," Colin cautioned, too weary to do much more. "Colleen, we came to you because we don't know who else to go to."

Noah returned with a tray of waters, passing them around. Catherine shoved hers away, nearly spilling it. Colin accepted his with a grateful, tight smile.

"I'll help, if I can," Colleen replied. Her pulse quickened. Whatever this was, it was no whim. Something was wrong... wrong enough she couldn't be sure there was anything she *could* do to help. She couldn't guess where this was going. Why they'd fled to her home, in the middle of the night, in their pajamas.

"Where's Oz?" Noah asked.

"At my mother's," Colin said.

"We'll pay for that later," Catherine murmured.

"All right," Colleen said. "So tell me what's wrong."

"It started, oh, maybe three months ago, wouldn't you say, Cat?"

"Now you're interested in what I have to say?"

Colin didn't even pretend to hide his annoyance with her. With a pointed look, he returned his gaze to Colleen. "I think it might have been happening to us both for a couple weeks before we ever talked about it. We both thought we were going crazy."

"That ship sailed long ago," Catherine said.

"We're used to crazy around here," Noah said, smiling. "So, a few months ago?"

"Yes, a few months ago, something strange started happening at night. I started seeing Oz in my dreams."

Catherine rolled her eyes.

"We both did, though we didn't talk about it for a while. Like I said, we both thought we were crazy."

"It's normal to see our loved ones in our dreams," Colleen said, though she knew this wasn't where Colin was going at all. Her dread deepened.

"No, that's not what this was." Colin kept shaking his head. He wrung his hands in his lap. He hadn't even bothered to comb his hair. "He's... it's more like he's an intruder. He doesn't belong there. I don't know how to explain it, except that he's not meant to be there."

"And it's like that with you, too?" Noah asked Catherine.

"It's like that," she said through a clenched jaw.

Colleen leaned back in her chair. She struggled for breath, as the realization started to, slowly, come over her. "You've never experienced anything else like this before? With anyone else? Ever?"

"No," the couple said in unison. "Never," Colin added.

"Dreamwalking," Colleen whispered, releasing a short, ragged breath with her words. "How unusual."

"I don't like the sound of that. Unusual," Catherine said.

"Well, it is unusual. I don't know any Deschanels who can do it," Colleen replied, shorter than she intended. Catherine's ill humor was rubbing off on her. She was tired. They all were.

"And? What does that mean, exactly?" Catherine demanded.

"I don't know," Colleen admitted. She looked at Noah for support, stifling a yawn, but he was subtly glaring at Catherine. "I don't know where Oz learned it. Why he can do it. Where he got it from, seeing as the rest of you are rather benign." She added that for Colin's benefit. She knew how the Sullivans felt about this topic.

"If you don't know, who would?" Colin asked. His tired eyes pleaded with her. "Who can help us?"

"What do you mean, help you? Train him?"

"Train him!" Catherine shrieked. "We want to stop him!"

"You want to stop him?" Colleen repeated, dumbfounded. But of course they wanted to stop him. The rest of the story filled in the blanks. They weren't here for guidance. They were here for an exorcism, of sorts. "I may not know a lot about dreamwalking, but I know everyone is born with something that makes him special."

"We don't want our son to be special like that, Colleen." Colin winced. "No offense."

"You can't say no offense and expect your words, which were intended to be offensive, not to be," Colleen said, and then shook her head, sighing. "It's late. We're all tired. Why don't we talk about this in the mor—"

Catherine shot up out of her chair. "You think we'd be here if we could sleep? We can't even *go* to sleep with our son in the same house anymore. It's completely out of control."

"Is he harming you in your dreams?"

"No, but—"

"No," Colleen said. "I didn't think so. Dreamwalking, from what I know, is relatively harmless. Have you tried just asking Oz not to do it?"

"Yes, we have," Colin replied. "We've tried talking to him

about it, but he thinks we're mad, so he just cries and says he doesn't know why it's happening." He pressed his lips together, controlling a wave of emotion. "He's not in control of himself when it's happening, Colleen, and it's breaking my heart."

"Does he understand when it's happening? The exact moment?"

"He just says he misses us," Catherine replied, calming some. "He misses us, and then he's with us. It's that simple to him. He doesn't know anything more than that."

"What if you brought him to sleep with the two of you?"

But as Colleen asked the question, she understood something they hadn't said. That there was a reason Oz pervaded their dreams individually. They slept in separate rooms. Perhaps had for a while.

"We just want it to stop," Catherine said quietly. "If anyone knows how to do that, it's you."

"Well, I don't know how," Colleen said. "And even if I did, I wouldn't help you."

The fire returned to Catherine's eyes. "Are you—"

Colleen held up a hand. "You didn't grow up the way I did. You didn't have to watch my sisters try and squelch their abilities. You didn't see Elizabeth struggle with a heavy drug problem. You haven't lived as I've lived."

"Maybe Elizabeth wouldn't have *had* a drug problem if someone had *helped* her," Catherine snapped.

Noah's steady hand on Colleen's shoulder stopped her from reaching across and slapping the woman. Colin's eyes flashed with apology.

She swallowed a hard breath and stood. "I think we're done here."

"Catherine didn't mean that," Colin said quickly. "We're just very tired. We're not sleeping much these days."

"She did mean it," Colleen said, with a heavy, knowing look at Catherine. "And tired or not, I can't help you."

"Can't or won't?" Catherine said under her breath.

"Does it matter? Do you even care about what I've said? You came here with a single mind. To change your son."

"That is not..."

"Yes," Colleen said firmly. "It is. This is part of who Oz is, whether you like it or not. This is no different than if you'd learned he was homosexual and tried to talk him out of that, too. He was born special, and one day, he'll die special. You can either learn to love him for who he is, or drown in your misery. I don't care."

Noah's eyes widened.

Colin's mouth flapped, searching for words. "I'm sorry. I didn't come here to start a fight."

"No, but your wife did," Colleen said. Silently, she pressed this thought into Catherine's head, so just the two of them could hear. *Don't ever come to my house again unless you intend to apologize.*

Catherine's hand flew to her mouth in shock.

"I'll walk you both out," Noah said, letting his hand brush against his wife's lower back as he closed the door behind him.

Would she tell him later, that she had another motive for shutting down their request?

It's fuzzy to me, Colleen, but some day Colin's kid is going to help save Amelia's life.

Oz?

He's the only kid they're gonna have. And he's important.

I don't understand, Lizzy. How?

I don't know, but he's... uh, well, he's got an ability, it seems. I couldn't see it all. I saw him with Amelia in a gazebo, at The Gardens, but not these *Gardens, if that makes sense. No, no, I know it doesn't, but I know it's important. I know you need to help Oz if his parents won't.*

She'd meant what she'd said, about not changing Oz. She would've given the same advice to anyone she cared about, no matter the circumstance.

But now she understood Elizabeth's words better.

She understood them well enough to know trying to squelch Oz's ability was bigger than two parents having bad dreams.

Amelia *was* an empath, and one day, she'd become imperiled because of that.

And one day, Oz would save her.

CHAPTER 15

Never Going Back Again

Olivia was over at Augustus' when Maureen got the package. Alain was sleeping. He was a good sleeper, and by the time she finished reading the contents, she was grateful for the solitude.

The package had no return address, but the postmark was local. There was a card on thick gold-leaf stock, embossed with an "LV." There was also something else, but she couldn't think about that just yet.

We thank your brother for taking out our trash, so we didn't have to.

Unsigned. Only the "LV" there to provide indication of the origin.

Trembling, she set the card aside and reached for the plastic bag. The growing dread turned her stomach over. She didn't understand, yet, but a part of her was beginning to piece this together.

Maureen screamed when she withdrew a scarf, covered in dried blood. She scrambled back and away from the cursed present, almost flipping over the back of the couch. The flecks of silver woven through red and green, but there was never so much red before. Never so much...

She knew that scarf. Jesus God, she knew that scarf.

We thank your brother for taking out the trash, so we didn't have to.

"No, no, no, no," Maureen whined, crab-walking herself into the corner, where she curled up, folding further into herself. "Charles, no. Noooooooo!"

Edouard entered the room. "Maureen. What is it? What's going on?"

"He killed him! Charles killed him!"

"Charles... I'm sorry. I don't understand." He helplessly paced before her, disturbed by her state, but unfocused. "What did Charles do?"

"You don't know what he's capable of," Maureen sobbed. "What he's done, for years!"

But Edouard did know, to some extent. They wouldn't be having this conversation if Charles wasn't capable of changing lives. Maureen looked up at him. "He killed Soren, Ed. That's what he did. He killed my Soren, and he did it to hurt me, and this is... this is the last time." Maureen choked on her tears. She pointed at the couch. At the card... and the scarf. "See for yourself!"

Edouard wandered toward the evidence in a daze. He read the card, turning it over, and then reached for the scarf... then recoiled, jumping back. "Jesus Christ."

"No, just my brother, playing God." Maureen rolled her head back and howled.

"LV? Who is LV?"

"LaViolette! Don't you understand? Don't you get it? Soren was an outcast! A black sheep! They're not *mad* at Charles, they're thrilled he did what they didn't have to!"

"But why..." Edouard wasn't getting it, but he was trying. "Maureen, why? Why would he, as you suggest, kill Soren? And why would his family ever be okay with that?"

Maureen slid herself up the wall until she was standing. "You think you know Charles, because he bullied you into marrying me? Well, you don't. You don't know what he's done. You wanna know why he did it? Why he does it? Because he *can,* Edouard. Because he can! Because he's past the point of having justified reasons to protect his family, so he's concocting them from thin air!"

"But—"

"Stop trying to wrap your head around it, you'll fail! Soren did what we asked, and everything was fine. He was fine, I was fine. We... well, I don't know what we are, but it had nothing to do with Charles, did it? But he needed a reason. A *fix.* He needed to fulfill his disgusting need to kill."

"How do we know Soren is really dead?"

Maureen coughed out a sound resembling a laugh. She thought it sounded like the laughter of a dead person. "I know. When you've grown up with a killer, you learn to appreciate his handiwork."

"None of this makes any sense! Why didn't the LaViolettes go to the police?"

"Have you even been listening? Soren has never fallen in line. Their family is even more clannish than mine. They expect everyone to play a role, and Soren refused. They let him live his life in obscurity, but they had to know about... about Alain..." Maureen rolled around, facing the corner, howling her agony into the plaster wall.

Seconds later, a heavy hand fell on her shoulder. It lacked warmth, but somewhere within him, Edouard meant this, this comfort.

"We should, then," he said, gathering his wits again. "We should go to the police."

"No," Maureen said quickly. She wiped at her eyes and turned. "I mean, yes. Maybe. But first I need to see my sister."

"Which one?"

"Colleen."

"I'm coming with you."

. . .

"Whoa, slow down, Maureen," Colleen called after her sister, who sprinted in a dead heat toward the parlor. Edouard hung behind, wearing an unreadable look. "Tell me again what Charles did?"

"He did it again, Colleen! Hell's bells, he can't even help himself anymore, can he?"

Colleen reached for her sister, but Maureen ripped herself away. Her face was a portrait of streaky black streaks and a graveyard of tears. "What are you talking about?"

Edouard went to the bar and poured Maureen a drink. He handed it to her, backing away to give her space. Colleen was as confused by this odd tenderness as Maureen's display, but she only had energy for one mystery.

"Charles," Maureen managed through her hyperventilation. She wrapped her hands around the whiskey glass to stabilize them, taking a shaky sip. Edouard reached forward to steady her. "He's done it again, Colleen. This time he's gone too far." Before she could explain, Maureen rolled to her side on the couch and lost herself to more sobbing.

Edouard cleared his throat. "We got a package today, Colleen. It seemed to infer—"

"No inferring!" Maureen screamed from the couch cushion.

Edouard set his lips with a short sigh. "It suggested that Charles had… had killed Soren LaViolette." He reached into his jacket and withdrew the card so Colleen could read for herself.

She dropped it as she took in the last words.

Colleen stepped back, inhaling her gasp. "He did not. Oh, God. Charles, Jesus Christ." If this was true, her brother had gone too far this time. Not like the first time wasn't too far, but this… a LaViolette. This was someone who would be missed. Someone who, no matter what the LaViolettes might say in their cryptic note, would demand recompense.

But more importantly, this was someone Maureen had loved. Someone who had loved her in return.

"There was also a scarf, covered in blood," Edouard explained.

"I don't understand, how did they get a scarf with his blood?"

"Soren's blood!" Maureen cried. "And they know everything, Colleen. They know more than us. They know everything and anything and everything!"

"Let me get her something from my medicine cabinet," Colleen offered, but Edouard shook his head.

"This anger is hers. She should feel it, if she wants to."

"The anger is only hurting *her.* She can't hurt Charles with it." Colleen closed her eyes, blowing out a breath. "No one can. Because nothing ever seems to hurt him. Not for long."

"I'm going to the police."

Colleen's eyes flew open. "Is that what Maureen wants?"

"If it is, you'll support her," Edouard demanded.

"I never said I wouldn't, but last time…" Colleen trailed off. Edouard may be family, but he was a stranger.

He curled the corner of his mouth into a bemused laugh. "She told me this wasn't his first. But don't you think it's our responsibility to make sure it's his last?"

"Our responsibility is to Maureen and her emotional health right now," Colleen said, turning again toward her sister. She knelt by her side. "Sweetie, tell me what you want to do."

"I want Charles to pay for this!"

"How? What does that look like for you?" Colleen tangled her hands through Maureen's which were drenched in tears. Her heart caved inward. "He's lost his mind, Maureen. I don't know what else to say, but he's a madman now. He's not the Charles we grew up with."

"He's always been this Charles, just now the dial goes to eleven," Maureen said coldly.

"What do you want to do?"

"You ask me that, but you already know you won't help me." Maureen ripped her hands away. "There you go, like you always do, talking to me like a goddamn child." She jumped off the couch and grabbed Edouard by the arm. "Come on, we're going to Ophélie. I want to look that bastard in the eyes and make him tell me what he did. I want him to say it!"

Edouard's wide eyes met Colleen's. She had no wisdom. Not anymore. Not about this.

"Let her go," Colleen said. "If she needs this, she needs this. We can't protect Charles from himself anymore. I'm not sure we ever should've tried, if this was going to be the consequence."

Edouard nodded, half-carrying Maureen as they left.

When they were gone, Colleen turned to find Noah standing on the stairs.

"How much did you hear?" she asked.

"Enough," he replied, descending. "Maybe it *is* time to stop protecting him."

"I don't know what to do."

"Why does it have to be you?"

"Maureen came to me. She could've gone to anyone else."

"Leena. She'll do what she feels is right. And if she decides to turn him in, you should let her. You should realize that some things are more important than family. Why should Charles be the only one who never has to learn the hard lessons? Why does he get to keep hurting others, simply because you all share the same ancestry?"

Colleen collapsed in his arms.

MAUREEN WAS OUT THE DOOR BEFORE EDOUARD stopped the car. He called after her, but she didn't stop, she couldn't stop. An energy unlike any she'd ever had propelled her forward, and there was no slowing it.

Cordelia's polite answering of the door faded to deep confusion as Maureen blew past her, screaming her brother's name.

"Hang on, let me get him," Cordelia offered, jogging up the stairs.

"You do that!"

Maureen paced the cypress, forcing herself to breathe through the erratic electricity radiating through her veins, out through her limbs. She was afraid she might combust, or take off, flying into the heavens, never to return.

"Maureen?" Charles wiped away sleep from his eyes. His matted hair drove her anger over the edge. A man who could sleep, after what he did!

"Look me in the eyes and tell me what you did!" she screamed before he'd made it down the stairs.

Charles paused at the center of the staircase. His hands dropped to his sides. "Excuse me?"

"Tell me what you fucking did, Charles!"

She felt Edouard step to her side, but he kept his silence.

"I just woke up from a goddamn nap, Maureen, so you'll need to be more speci—"

"Soren!" she yelled. And then again, and again. There was power in saying his name. A power born in love, and now, death. "My Soren!"

Cordelia's jaw dropped. "Charles. You didn't."

"Like you fucking know anything," he hissed at her, descending a couple more steps. His bare feet gripped the old patterned carpet, as if rooting himself in place in defense. "Maureen, let's go in the parlor, and we can talk there."

"I'm not going anywhere with you now, or ever again!" she cried out. "And anything we're going to say is good enough for our spouses, wouldn't you say, Huck? Wouldn't you say that if someone is going to commit a crime they should be willing to own it? Not run away from it?"

A visible change came over her brother. His façade melted, replaced by annoyance. "Jesus, Maureen, I wasn't the one having babies with my fucking lover now, was I?"

"Don't put this on Maureen," Edouard said, tensing at her side. She almost loved him then. She could almost forget what he, too, had done to her.

"And you?" Charles took another step down. "I should take admonishments from you, the rapist?"

"I know the wrong I've done your sister. Do you?"

"Wrong?" Charles repeated, cackling. "All I do, all I do is look after my family, and *I'm* the bad guy? Me?"

Cordelia looked up at him. "Come on, Charles. Doesn't it get exhausting? Pretending that's why you do it?"

"Fuck you, Cord."

"She's right, Charles. She might be the cunt who once kidnapped our Lizzy, but she's right about this," Maureen said. "She's had your number all along, hasn't she?"

"You want me to tell the world? I'll scream it from the rooftops, Maureen." Charles leaned his head back, spreading his arms. "Yes, world, I did it! Once again, I fucking took care of my family's problems, and once again, they come not to thank me but to cry about it! To fucking *whine* about problems they created and I fixed! Yes, I killed Soren! I killed that fucking teacher! I killed the assholes who raped Evie! I killed the professor who took advantage of Colleen, and when that bitch married Au—"

"Stop before you say—" Cordelia warned, but there was no stopping Charles.

"Ekatherina was a fucking cancer to our brother, and I was the only one with the goddamn balls to do something about it."

Maureen's horror deepened, cutting a wide path around her, one that, though she didn't realize it then, would become permanent.

Her brother wasn't a misguided protector.

He was a monster.

"He didn't mean that," Cordelia said, barely above a whisper.

"Oh, he meant it," Maureen said, backing away so quickly she stumbled. "He meant every word. He's always meant it. He always will."

"Go on, tell our pussy of a brother! I don't fucking care! What's he going to do, Maureen? What are you going to do? Nothing! Nothing, and that's always been the fucking problem, and *why you needed me*!"

Charles beat his chest with the words, and at last Maureen knew coming here was a mistake, but she could unwind it.

She could unwind Charles from her life.

She could unwind it all, along with her love for a man who would never see justice for his murder.

"You're dead to me," she said as she fell out the front door. "You are not Alain's godfather. You'll never see *any* of us again."

Edouard caught her on the porch and held her close to his chest as she released the last of her sobs into his unexpected, but welcome strength.

COLLEEN WAS STILL SO SHAKEN UP FROM HER FIRST visitor that the second one caught her off guard.

Elizabeth's face was heavy as she let herself in, walking past Colleen.

"Maureen found out about Soren, didn't she?"

Colleen paced around the front of her sister. "You knew? You knew and said nothing?"

"When has knowing ever changed anything?" Elizabeth moved toward the screened porch, Colleen in tow. "Maureen deserves so much better than the life she's been given. Knowing that doesn't give her a path to a better one, either, though."

"Is that why you're here?"

Elizabeth turned around and faced Colleen, dropping into the wicker chair with a soft thud. "No, actually."

"Should we talk about it? We need to rally around Maureen, to give her all the support we can offer."

"She won't take it, Colleen," Elizabeth said, rocking lightly. "She'll never take anything from any of us ever again."

Colleen sat across from her, leaning forward on her knees. "A guess? Or a premonition?"

"I've seen it. What Charles did is the final tear in the fabric of this family. Why it was this, and not a million other things, only God knows, I suppose."

"You don't normally confess your premonitions with me. Why now?"

"To make a point."

"And what point is that?"

"I could be of use to you. To the Council."

"Oh, Lizzy, not this again, and not today, of all days."

"Yes, today, of all days." Elizabeth stopped rocking. "I'm going to tell you something, Colleen. I know I did this once before, and it's changed you, and I'm sorry for that, but if telling you about what happened to me in Paris sets us on the right course, then maybe it's worth it."

"What happened to you in Paris?"

"I met someone." Elizabeth cleared her throat. "He said his name was Tristan, but I know that isn't who he is, not really. Or what he is. But he knows who we are. It's more than that, he's a part of us, in some way. Maybe a guardian angel. Maybe... I don't know. It's not fair to speculate."

Colleen frowned. "Tristan. Won't that be your son's name, one day?"

"It will," Elizabeth said. "And all because of this one night in Paris."

Elizabeth then told her a story. Of joy and love, followed by fear and angst. Of one desperate moment that almost cost Connor his life. And of a stranger, one she'd seen before, who not only saved him but offered Elizabeth a gift no one else had ever offered her.

"He asked me if I wanted to know the exact hour and manner of my death."

Colleen's heart nearly beat out of her chest. "And did you? Accept?"

Elizabeth nodded. "I did."

"Oh, God." Colleen clutched her chest. She'd never doubted Lizzy's visions, but to have them independently confirmed, and by a mysterious stranger that had never once blipped on their radar. And the detail... the detail, somehow, filled in the last blanks in the tapestry. It removed all semblance of reasonable doubt. "And?"

Elizabeth shook her head. "No, sorry. It's enough for me to live with it. I won't put that on you, too."

"But... I mean, it's not..."

"Not that soon, no." Elizabeth smiled. "Soon enough, I suppose. Sooner than I would've liked."

"Why tell me, then?"

"Because I need you to understand I'm not little Lizzy who can't handle her visions anymore, Colleen. I'm wounded, but I'm not broken. Bent, not destroyed. If I can live with knowing exactly when and why I'll die, then you can find it in you to trust that not only am I capable of taking a seat next to you and the others, but I may actually be the missing link you've needed all along. Maybe I'm not the weak one, Colleen."

Elizabeth got out of her chair. She knelt in front of Colleen. "Maybe I've always been the strong one. Maybe it's time you put that strength to work for us."

WINTER 1980

NEW ORLEANS, LOUISIANA
VACHERIE, LOUISIANA

CHAPTER 16

As It Always Was

"Repeat after me," Colleen commanded. "In power, obligation."

Elizabeth swallowed. "In power, obligation."

"In obligation, commitment."

"In obligation, commitment."

"In commitment, solidarity."

"In commitment, solidarity."

"In solidarity," Colleen finished, "enlightenment."

Elizabeth pressed her sweaty hands under the table. "In solidarity, enlightenment."

"You know those vows as the ones all members of the Collective say upon swearing in, and at the start of every meeting. But I have one more for you, Elizabeth. One just for the Council, and while the words are simple, they are weighted with hundreds of years of gravity."

Elizabeth nodded. "I'm ready."

"Then repeat, with me, these final words. That, as a member of this esteemed Council, you vow to achieve the gravity of this governance as an extension of your enlightenment. 'Governance, through enlightenment.'"

"Governance," Elizabeth said, wondering when the chambers had grown so warm. "through enlightenment."

Colleen smiled. "Very good. Now, we are again whole." She smiled at the other five who'd been watching the swearing-in. "I trust you'll all make Elizabeth most welcome. This Council has seen a complete transformation in these past five years. All young blood now, and no old guard. Pansy, Kitty, and I are the oldest ones here, and not a one of us is thirty."

Pansy laughed. "God help us all."

"I appreciate everyone's vote of confidence," Elizabeth said as she let her eyes fall on her fellow Council members. Three sisters, and the rest, cousins she hardly knew. Pansy, Kitty, Luther, Jasper. She had no qualms with any of them, but it seemed odd to her that she would now be joined with them in the most sacred responsibility the family had. She had so many questions for Colleen, but had been so afraid her older sister would change her mind that she let them all die unasked. But still... did they get along? Did they all share a vision? How often did they vote on things, and how often did the voting lead to a stalemate?

"Now, we're more balanced," Kitty said. "I know Colleen was feeling awful lonely up there until Evangeline came along, and it only seemed right to bring in another from the heir's line. But don't be thinking this is some kind of party."

Evangeline rolled her eyes.

"No, that wasn't my expectation," Elizabeth assured her.

"Good, because it isn't like Congress or nothing," Pansy said.

"If it was Congress, I would've run the opposite direction," Elizabeth said, smiling. "Anyway, I didn't come here for fun and games. I'm a wife now, and I know I'll be a mother when it's time. I want to serve this family, like I told Colleen. Isn't there some expression about service to others being its own reward or something?" She shook her head. She was rambling. Time to refocus. "I know that, other than some hard losses, we've been lucky. I know about the Curse, and as a seer, I can't stop it, but perhaps I can help better prepare us for it."

"Our first seer on the Council," Luther said. "Of course, other than Ophelia."

"How did she use her gifts here?" Elizabeth asked.

Pansy shrugged. "She didn't. She'd act like she didn't have 'em, for the most part. You know, sometimes she'd prepare us for some vague, obscure thing, but she ain't never come out and say, one of y'all gonna die, or nothing like that."

Elizabeth turned to Colleen. "Maybe there are rules about it, for the Council. Did she ever say?"

"No," Colleen replied, with a thoughtful look at Ophelia's portrait on the wall. "Not really, but the thing about Ophelia was, that wasn't her way. You have to remember that she resurrected this tradition from France, and she built it from nothing but notes and memories of others. All by herself. And then when she started bringing in family to help, she was still running it. Still the only one who really *believed* in what we were. Even when I joined, our meetings were still mostly perfunctory. A sense of limbo, as if we were waiting... for *something*. The Curse, maybe, or something else, but she said to me before she died that she could only do so much to make the Council what it was, and that we, this generation, all of us, had to take it where it was meant to go."

Their peers in the room each absorbed this in their own way, some nodding, others staring off into the distance.

"Would you *like* me to use my ability here?" Elizabeth pressed.

"I want to do what Ophelia set the foundation for us to do," Colleen said. "I want to build our network of witches, and I want us to improve attendance at Collective meetings. I want us to truly lead in a way she knew she couldn't do without the buy-in not only of her Council, but the broader family. We've existed on islands for too long. It's time for us to come together." Colleen nodded at the Council. "We're starting down that path now, Elizabeth. Luther has our first gathering on the calendar for the new year, and we're going to start putting more interesting topics on the agendas to elicit interest from the rest of the Deschanels,

Fontenots, Guidrys, and so on. To answer your question... I want you to only ever use your power with those goals in mind. And only then, if you think it will help bring us closer together, and not further apart."

When the others were gone, Elizabeth lingered. "What changed your mind?" she asked Colleen, as their sister closed the door. They'd said goodbye to Evangeline, who was flying back to Switzerland, and would be home again soon for Christmas.

"Oh, I don't know..."

Elizabeth reached for her sister's hands. "I want to know."

"Tristan," Colleen blurted, and when Elizabeth's confusion stole over her face, she quickly corrected herself. "No, not him, specifically, but your encounter with him. It has to mean something."

"I don't think his name is really Tristan," Elizabeth replied.

"You don't believe him?"

"I believe him about the important things. But he even said as much, about his name, that he'd given it to me because I was meant to one day give it to my son. But I don't think his real name, or who he was, was all that important to the events of that night, and *why* he was there. Whoever he is, he doesn't need us to know anything else about him in order to protect us."

"And you think that's what he is to us. A protector."

"Maybe? I don't know. I saw him watching me in Paris, and I'd never seen him before that. And I'd remember, Colleen, because this guy..." Elizabeth laughed. "He's beautiful. Gorgeous, with this oddly colored red and silver hair. But my God, this man doesn't belong in this century, he belongs in a museum. The way he dresses, talks, acts. And he wears a sword that probably came from the goddamn Viking invasion of the British Isles."

Colleen frowned. "That is odd. Ophelia never mentioned anything like that."

"He doesn't look any older than me, but I have a feeling he's been looking after us a good long while."

"But that doesn't make any sense."

"No, but not much about who we are ever has, has it? We've never asked ourselves why we're this way. Where it comes from."

"And you think this Tristan has something to do with that?"

"I don't know anything at all, other than the man thought it was a priority to protect my future. *Our* future. He mentioned that, you know, what I'd told you. About Tristan, my Tristan that is, saving the family one day."

"He did? He said that?"

"He reminded me what was at stake."

"And where was this protector when Maddy died?"

Elizabeth shook her head. "I don't think it works like that, Colleen. I think that it's like... like questioning why God lets children die. We all have free will, and that's part of us, but our path has already been set. Free will is a construct. Maybe this is a chicken and egg argument, but it's hard to say whether our choices made by free will are what set us on this predetermined path, or whether this path backed us into those choices. I'm not good with philosophy. But I believe all the choices we make, we were destined to make. Free will be damned, the choices might be ours, but they were already written before we made them."

"But why would he save Connor? By that logic, wasn't Connor always meant to jump? And haven't we always known that we can't change the future?"

Elizabeth shook her head. "Because Connor *wasn't* supposed to die that night. His decision to do that was affected by my attempt to alter the timeline. Me threatening to change the future went against the natural order of things, something only a seer, oddly, would be capable of doing. Tristan created a paradox of sorts, in correcting us back to the course that was meant for us, which, in its own way, also changed the future. Because in doing so, he's changed me, and now I'm on the path that led me to you."

"That's very confusing," Colleen said, but her expression was interested. She wanted to know more. She wanted to understand.

"Do you think all seers have a Tristan? What would stop them from throwing the future off course without one?"

Elizabeth shrugged. "Maybe they do. Maybe Ophelia knew him, by another name and another set of circumstances. Or someone like him. When she let me go on that fool's errand to try and stop the ship from wrecking, it was obvious then she knew I wouldn't, couldn't change it, but there was also an odd glint in her eye. I didn't understand it then. Maybe I do now. Our only real power as a seer is the one we have over life and death with ourselves."

"Don't you wish you could ask him?"

"Oh, aye," Elizabeth said, using Tristan's word, and his strange way of talking. "But the one thing I do know about the man is we'll never meet again, not in this life. He told me so, and I have no reason not to believe him."

CHARLES GAVE UP THE GLASS AN HOUR AGO, NOW taking swigs directly from the bottle of Hennessey on his desk. His smoldering cigarette prepared for death in his ashtray, but he still had more, another pack, and he'd smoke them all because there was no one who cared enough to stop him from that, or the heavy drinking. When he'd kicked the cocaine, he'd done it all by himself. And wasn't that the real Deschanel curse? The curse of the heir? How lonely it was at the top, when you had to make all the decisions, do all the protecting so others could live in peace?

That Fontaine man had been his first kill to protect himself. He thought of it as a gift, but it didn't matter, it was his favorite one yet, because he'd done it to satisfy his own self, not correct the wrongdoing against a loved one. He'd drawn it out, way out, enjoying thoroughly the fear and confusion in the man's eyes as Charles choked him hard enough to pull him away from the world, but not hard enough to do it quickly and with mercy. His cock grew hard even thinking of it.

When he'd eventually released Fontaine—whose first name

he'd never bothered to remember—the man's bloodshot eyes protruded so far they no longer closed. Charles tried to close them, because he didn't like that red-eyed look the old foreman kept giving him, but no dice. They were burst like an overripe grape. Probably a closed casket, unless the funeral home had better luck.

Angelique's letter lay crumpled on his desk. He had half a mind to burn it and send it back to her, but he feared *any* response would only incite her. He didn't know why he hadn't seen it when he was fucking her into oblivion, but the woman was completely certifiable, in a way that scared him senseless. She continued her threats. Continued pleading for him to make her his wife and bring her to Ophélie. God's pajamas! None of the other women he'd fucked had ever dreamed so big, or dared so loudly. Because they knew better. They knew their place and knew his. They knew what it was and what it wasn't.

But not Angelique. He'd increased the checks, and she'd only upped her demands. She had a son, and now a child on the way, and Charles had a responsibility. So, Charles set up a goddamn college fund for the Jesse kid, who wasn't even his, and another for the unborn child who was. He increased the payments once more. He wondered why she still lived in a shack, when she had over half a million dollars of his money. He had no idea what she wanted.

Same as you. Power.

Charles didn't know where that errant thought had come from, but he pushed it back, as he did with all uncomfortable truths.

But he had his own truth now. There would soon be at least two children out in the world, bearing his genetics. Only he could stem this tide. Just as it had been his decision to kick the coke, it had to be his to put aside his addiction with women. He didn't need them now, anyway, did he? They were all the same. They bored him. What didn't bore him was his newfound interest in business. There was always something new to learn, to discover.

That hopefulness he'd had with women had been replaced, and now, thanks to Angelique, killed. He'd always been a protector, but his means of doing so had shifted. That's all.

An empire. He'd take their billionaire status and double it. Triple it. What came after billions? He'd do that.

"Ah, there you are," Cordelia said, stepping only into the doorway of his third floor office. She waved her hand around. "How long have you been in here? I'm surprised the fire alarm hasn't gone off."

"Funny," he muttered, stubbing out what was left of his smoke. "Did you need something?"

"We haven't finished our Christmas shopping this year."

"You know I don't give a shit about that stuff. What do you even give people who already have everything? Don't we usually give the meaningless gift of money, anyway?"

"The children, Charles. They're little. They don't care about money. They still enjoy the mountains of presents under the tree."

Despite his wealth, Charles hadn't experienced that. His mother was careful not to indulge them, despite his father's inclination to do exactly that. "Well, I don't know, what do other kids love right now? Uh, yeah, those weird cabbage dolls. Get them that."

"They already have Cabbage Patch Dolls. And I already bought everything on their list for them."

Charles shook another cigarette from the pack and lit it. "So, what's the problem then?"

"Don't you want to be a part of these years, Charles? Don't you want to pick something out, so when they open it, you can say you saw it and thought of them?"

"Why would I do that?"

Cordelia sighed. "All right. I've got it covered, then."

"Don't sigh like that at me. Like I've disappointed you or something."

"Not me," Cordelia said.

"I'm building a future for them! Isn't that enough?"

"One day, maybe," she said. "Right now, they don't understand. All they know is their father is away all the time. Nicolas is the only one who gets regular affection, and it took us shipping him to New Orleans to get it." Cordelia smiled, seemingly to herself. "I know my weaknesses, too, darling. I know what I'm good at and not. But I *am* trying, with your girls. Don't ask me why... I don't know. Maybe because I was terrible to their mother, or maybe it's penance, or maybe... it doesn't matter. But I'm not their mother. They know this. And I'm definitely not their father."

"Well, you are a bit mannish."

"Charles."

He rolled his eyes. "Fine. You'll be happy to know I've given up women."

"Why would that make me happy, exactly?" She nodded at the paper. "It was that crazy bitch in Abbeville, wasn't it? Well, someone like her was bound to come along at some point and humble you."

"Not just her," Charles said. "Women are a distraction. I have goals now. Real ones."

"I see," Cordelia said. "Well, here's a goal for you, Charles. One you should take to heart."

He looked at her.

"Figure out what you want from life. What you *really* want. Because I think you've spent thirty-odd years bouncing from one shiny thing to the next and don't have a clue what happiness means."

COLLEEN RAN HER HANDS THROUGH AMELIA'S LONG white hair, which was stretched across her lap along with her daughter. Noah had both the boys with him, Ashley in his arms, Ben curled around at his side. His sleepy expression was lit by dancing colors of the exterior Christmas lights, which had gone up only a few nights earlier. The Gardens would be an array of seasonal showmanship until the new year, as it always was.

As it always was. These words had played an important role in Colleen's considerations since the summer, when she'd moved her family home.

When she was younger, Colleen assumed—wrongly, she now understood—her family needed something only she could offer. That she was there to save them from themselves, to guide the moral center of the blood. Further harmful was her belief that her own meaning and place in this world could only be achieved through these means, and that to fail at this would mean to fail utterly.

"You went somewhere," Noah said softly from his rocker. "Just now, in your head."

"I'm always going somewhere."

"Somewhere from before."

She smiled. "You always know. I was thinking about the past, I guess. How much has changed."

Noah kissed both his sons, gently so as not to wake them. "Everything, you could say."

"Everything that matters." She wound Amelia's soft hair through her fingers. "I'm glad we came back when we did, Noah. But not before, is what I mean. That we waited. That we focused on us before we came back to the real world."

"Nothing was ever more real to me than our years in Scotland," Noah said. "But I understand what you're saying. I'm glad, too. Everything is as it should be."

"As it always was," she whispered. "I don't have big visions for my family anymore, but I do have them for *the* family. If that makes sense."

"It does. The Council."

"The Council." Colleen leaned back in her chair. Her sweet Amelia stirred in her lap. "I want to make Ophelia proud."

"I think you already have, love."

"I hope so. But I always feel as if I'm chasing her vision, guessing at what she would've wanted, playing a game almost."

"But wasn't her vision for you to create your own?" Noah asked, and it broke Colleen completely from her reverie.

"My own?"

"That never occurred to you?"

"Well, yes, to some degree, but..." Colleen pulled the blanket up over her daughter. She'd been so accustomed to Ophelia's tendency to communicate in riddles that she thought her charge upon her great-aunt's death was to decipher one final, critical one. That of the future of the Council. But what if she'd had it wrong all along, and Ophelia's final test had been one that only Colleen could set for herself?

And hadn't she done this already? Letting Luther fly with his ideas? Letting Jasper work on new agendas? Breathing new life, new ideas. Was this what was meant all along?

"I love you, Colleen."

Colleen looked up, drawn to the seriousness in her husband's voice.

"What's wrong?" she asked, instinctively. Because she could never, even now, quite shake the idea that real affection only preceded tragedy.

"Nothing," he said with a soft, languid smile. "Only that I'm going to keep saying that, as much as I need to, until one day when you look up you'll know everything is as it should be."

CHAPTER 17
Second Chances

On order of the family priest, Augustus kissed his bride for the second time in his life. Unlike the first, where he'd been nervous and inexplicably smitten, this time he was content. Barbara's pretty smile, full of the same happiness but devoid of expectations, greeted him when he pulled back, set to the applause of their immediate families.

Colleen had insisted on hosting them at The Gardens. Although they'd only invited their closest loved ones, Colleen had nonetheless gone to some trouble to make the setting lovely and ornate, even in the cool throes of winter. She'd wound all sorts of red and pink flowers Augustus recognized but could never name around the trellis and found a roll of crimson satin for the aisle. He wanted to tell her none of this was necessary for the type of marriage he and Barbara signed up for, but that wasn't entirely true about the marriage. Practical though it may be, it was an investment in both their futures. It was a gamble, that two people looking for the non-traditional could find a traditional sort of happiness. Augustus needed a caretaker, and Barbara, someone for whom to care for, and if fate was kind, this would be the recipe for their own individual happiness.

And Ana's.

She'd looked so pretty, skipping down the aisle in her pink chiffon gown, spreading the white flowers and seeds around with flourish. When her aunt Elizabeth reached over to smooth a lump in her dress, she'd unsmoothed it just as fast, swelling with pride at her important role.

She seemed to like Barbara. Augustus thought it was too soon to predict his new wife might become a replacement mother, but that wasn't entirely what he was after, anyway. What he wanted was a maternal figure, someone who could guide Ana through the tough things fathers struggled with—especially fathers like Augustus, who struggled through anything requiring more complex emotions. It wouldn't be long before Ana experienced changes he had no qualifications to help her through. But Barbara did.

Unlike Ekatherina, who'd wilted in the face of familial affection, Barbara blossomed. She left Augustus' side, not needing his help to mingle with her new family. She was charming and lovely, and for a fleeting moment he worried that her decision to marry a man who was really neither of those things might turn to regret. But he and Barbara were similar creatures, in that once they'd made their mind up they seemed to commit to the direction, whatever it was. They understood each other in that way.

And, while this hadn't even been a gleam in his mind at the time, she'd satisfied another need, one he hadn't really known he had. She was generous in the bedroom, and without the fear of leaving her with child, he could be generous, too. With Ekatherina, he'd embraced each of these experiences with the creeping fear she'd turn away. That she'd run away. He could enjoy himself with Barbara, who'd come to him with a practicality that was almost sexy. Their needs could both be fulfilled, without losing who they were.

It was a surprise to Augustus, to learn he enjoyed sex. He'd always experienced an almost indignant pride at being a man not vulnerable to the needs other men had. But Barbara was only the fourth woman he'd been with. The first time, with Carolina, had been fumbling and strange. The second, with Ekatherina, with an eye, always, to his fear of disappointing her. Then the woman in the bathroom... well, he *had* enjoyed that, and his enjoyment brought him shame, as if he'd tapped into a dark part of himself never meant to be surfaced. But Barbara gave without fear of the bigger picture, and he was learning to do the same.

Elizabeth slipped her arm through his, leaning against him. "I like her."

"Yeah?"

"Yeah. She reminds me of you, but also..."

"You can say it."

"Maddy," Elizabeth finished. "There's a light in her. I hope it never goes out."

"Ana likes her, too."

"That's important." Elizabeth unwound herself and turned to face him. "Ana will have her struggles, Aggie. I've told you that I've seen some of them. She'll be happy in the end, but it won't always be easy for her, and she's going to need her family. She has a natural tendency to isolate, but it's important you don't let her do it too much. You both have so many people who love you, and who are only a phone call away." She strained on her tiptoes to kiss his cheek. "But this is a happy day. Be happy, Augustus. You deserve it."

EVANGELINE DROPPED HER BAG ON THE COUNTER OF Johannes' small apartment. He looked up, from where he was cooking. Salmon. She picked up the scent of dill.

"Ahh, welcome back," he said, craning his neck back to kiss her. "How was home?"

"Marry me," she said. She backed away, into the counter opposite.

Johannes' spatula hovered in the air as he froze, head to toe.

"*Förlåt*?"

"Beautiful man, you know I don't speak Swedish."

"Did you say what..."

"Turn around, Viking."

"Evangeline."

"Turn around."

Johannes set his utensil to the side and slowly did as she asked. She held out a small gold band. She'd picked it up in New Orleans, from the place where Augustus had an account, where he'd foolishly bought the ring for Ekatherina. Before she'd left Switzerland, she'd wrapped a string around her future husband's ring finger to get the right measure, while he was sleeping. Science, and all that.

"I love you. You love me. Let's make babies."

Johannes' eyes filled with tears. "What a proposal this is."

"You're lucky, Viking. I had a whole speech prepared that would have made us *both* wish for the part where we skip to the end and you say yes."

"You seem so sure my answer would be yes."

"I know it will." She flipped her heavy curls. "Who could resist the opportunity for a mess like me for the rest of their lives?"

"You are perfection in the chaos," Johannes said, no longer smiling. He stepped forward and his hands came up, hesitating only a moment before winding them through her impossible hair. "You are my mess."

"Is that a yes?"

"Aren't you supposed to be on your knees?"

"Skipping right to the good part, are we?"

Johannes' eyes flew wide as he took her meaning. "Well, while you're down there..."

Evangeline kissed him. "Marry me, Johannes Gehring. I don't want anyone else. You've ruined me for anyone else. I love you that much."

"Took you far too long to ask." He kissed her back. "I knew the day I met you."

"That wasn't an invitation to show off, sheesh."

"Well, I did. I knew there was something different about you. Something I could love. I want a life with you, too, Evangeline."

"So just say yes so we can have sex already!"

"Yes! Yes, yes, yes!" he cried, laughing, as he swept her into his arms. "But, we're adults and adults don't burn good salmon. Great minds learn to multitask," he said as he settled her on the counter, flipping the fish with one hand, unbuckling her jeans with the other.

"I YELLED AT OLIVIA TODAY," MAUREEN SAID, SITTING across the kitchen table from Augustus. She'd been so nervous, setting up what seemed like such a formal meeting with her own brother. He'd told her that Barbara and Ana were at Barbara's mother's for the afternoon, and Maureen knew then that today would be the day she worked up the courage to ask for help.

But first, small talk. She had to calm down.

"Why?" Augustus poured more hot water in her teacup.

"She's… predicting things. Like Lizzy."

"Oh. Wow." Augustus leaned back in his chair. Yes, wow, she thought. They both knew what this meant. They'd both seen the effects on Elizabeth. "What did you say to her?"

"To never, ever do it again," Maureen said. "Hell's bells, what was I supposed to do?"

"I would've done the same," Augustus said. "But I don't know if telling her that helps. Elizabeth has never been able to turn it off."

"A few months ago, she pointed at John Lennon when he was on the television and said he was going to get shot outside his apartment. She said those words, Augustus. Shot outside his apartment. I take it you saw the news a couple weeks ago?"

Augustus exhaled. "And that wasn't the first time?"

"Oh, no. So far she only seems to do it with strangers, or celebrities. Not like Lizzy, who was always seeing bad things happen to us." Maureen sighed. "But maybe she just isn't telling me all of it. She knows how upset I get."

"Maybe Elizabeth can help her."

Maureen shook her head. "I want her to focus on other things. Living, for one. If she does that, maybe it *will* go away. Mine did."

Augustus blinked. "You had an ability? All this time?"

She waved her hand. "Yes, but it's gone and doesn't matter now."

"What was it?"

"It really doesn't matter anymore, Aggie."

"How did none of us know that?"

"Charles did," Maureen said. "But... well, Charles is why I came over today. Why I wanted to talk to you."

Augustus folded his hands over the table. "All right. What's on your mind?"

"I don't know how much you know. About my relationship with Soren LaViolette."

Augustus looked down. "I knew about it, or at least, that there was one. I left it alone. It wasn't my business. I was so sorry to hear he disappeared, though."

"He's Alain's father. He didn't disappear. Charles killed him."

Augustus' head shot up so fast she thought he might jump out of his chair. "He what?"

"After all these years? Are you really surprised? Really?"

"But... after that... teacher... he promised me."

Maureen laughed. "Bless your heart, you think he stopped there?" She held up her fingers, ticking off. "Mr. Evers. Evangeline's attackers. Four, I think? Colleen's teacher." She paused, stopping herself before she could add what she knew about Ekatherina. But she didn't come here to hurt her brother, only solicit his guidance. "That's six, and then you add in Soren, and now the husband of that woman he was fucking—"

"What woman?"

"Does it matter?"

"I guess not, but... are you certain?"

"Yes, and what's more, I think you already knew all of this."

"I make it a point not to get involved in Charles' decisions, Maureen. It's better that way."

"Yes, and meanwhile he's left a trail of at least eight bodies and no one has done a thing. Not a thing!"

Augustus inhaled and held the breath, closing his eyes.

Maureen had kept the tears at bay, but she couldn't, not any longer. She'd tried so hard not to cry for Soren. For her sweet man. Her mad lover. Father of her son. She'd done this because if she succumbed to her grief and rage, there was no telling what the aftermath might look like. How her family would suffer.

But it ate away at her, just the same.

Day after day.

Night after night.

With Evers, she'd been a child, angry and indignant. With Soren, she'd been a woman, happily in love. Happy, even, to surrender that love for family, because she knew he still existed in the same world as her. Still looked up at the same stars, breathed the same air.

And Charles had stolen that, too, from her.

As he'd stolen her trust, those years ago with Evers.

As he'd stolen her innocence, forcing her into a marriage with her rapist.

And as he'd now stolen her joy.

These things had a way of wearing at the corners, of the very fabric of who she was. Maureen hadn't ever thought of herself as strong, but she understood, now, that she'd been strong all along. Stronger than any of them. But strong people didn't abide the actions of those weaker and crueler. They didn't allow their power, and power of others, to be continuously stolen by a callous bully.

"I believe you," Augustus said, his whole body animated through his heavy exhale. "You came to me for a reason."

"Colleen and Evangeline still act like Charles is a problem

they can't be bothered with. Like… like we just have to *live* with this! You know, it's just the way he is. But what happens, Augustus, when Colleen and Noah have a fight one day, and Charles finds out? What happens when Connor steps out of line? Do you know how many times he's offered to kill Edouard? Every day, I have to live with knowing he might. That we live in a reality where my own brother might very well kill my husband."

"Okay." Augustus seemed to be working hard to compose himself, to catch up to all the bombs she'd dropped on him in the space of minutes. "What do you want to do?"

"I want him to be accountable. I want him to stop."

"What does that look like to you?"

Maureen hesitated before saying the words. "I want to turn him in."

Augustus glanced at the clock. "We have a few hours before Barbara and Ana are home. That should be enough time to get down to the station and make a statement."

"You mean it?"

"Yes, Maureen." Augustus wiped his palm over his face, sighing. "I won't cover any of this up for him, not anymore. Maybe I've been intentionally ignorant, but I really didn't know it had come to this. I thought being a father… well, I thought he had better sense than this. And if he's hurting people like Soren, who've done nothing wrong, then he's spinning out of control. Whether he deserves punishment is between him and God, but we've all enabled this behavior for too long."

Maureen's tears spilled unabated now. A powerful relief, months in the making, washed over her, rendering her dizzy. "You'll really go with me to the police?"

"I will."

She realized she was shaking when Augustus reached across the table to steady her hand.

"It will be okay."

. . .

Augustus shifted in the cracked plastic chair at the police station. Beside him, Maureen was wound so tight he wondered if she might take off like a spaceship.

It wasn't that he didn't know what Charles was capable of. If anyone did, it was the brother who'd once been his closest friend. He wasn't naïve enough to think the teacher was the only one, and when he suspected Charles' involvement in the deaths of those homeless kids, he'd done some light smoothing with the authorities. But what Maureen described was horrifying. This wasn't a man protecting his family. This was a man spiraling into madness.

No, not spiraling there. Living there.

He'd always struggled with his role in protecting Charles from his actions. At the time, it had seemed they had no other choice. With Evers, everything had happened so fast, and they had to make a decision. Over time, the wound festering between him and Charles faded, and he could almost forget that once upon a time his brother had killed a man. But he hadn't forgotten, he'd just allowed himself to live in a world where people could change.

In turning his back, Augustus, too, was complicit. He didn't know if helping Maureen hold their brother accountable could make up for that, but if any of them deserved closure, it was Maureen.

"Mr. Deschanel? Mrs. Blanchard?" A detective in a brown suit stood before them. "I'm Detective Thompson. Follow me."

Maureen rose from her chair in a daze, wandering forward like a zombie. Augustus put a steadying hand on her shoulder and fought back his fears about what today's visit to the police might bring down upon their entire family.

"Have a seat," Detective Thompson said, as he closed the door to a small room. There was only a brown laminate table and three chairs, like the ones in the waiting area. Augustus had to nudge Maureen to snap her from the strange reverie she'd fallen into. "You said you had information regarding the disappearance of Soren LaViolette?"

"Yes, well, um..." Maureen wrung her hands. Beads of moisture appeared at her brow. "I'm sorry, I was wrong. I didn't mean to waste your time!" She bolted from the room, leaving Augustus to share a confused look with the detective.

"Sorry, she's not herself right now," Augustus said, before following her.

He found her outside, one hand on a bench, keeling over as if ready to retch.

"Maureen, what was that? What's going on?"

"I can't do it," she said, heaving over the back of the bench.

Augustus rubbed the center of her back, confused. "Breathe. Just breathe." When she was finally calm, he eased her onto the bench. "I don't understand what just happened in there."

"I couldn't do it."

"Why?"

Maureen's splotchy face turned to him. "Why? Because it's not just about him anymore, is it? I love Nicolas and the girls. What happens to them when their father goes to prison and their name is tainted in New Orleans? What future will they have, the heirs of a family whose name has been reduced to terrible violence?" She wiped at her eyes. "What happens to Mama when she has to watch her oldest son spend the rest of his life in prison, in disgrace?"

"Charles should have thought of those things before he did what he did."

"But he didn't," Maureen said, sniffling. "Because he never does. And if I do this, our whole family unravels. Everything. All of it. All of us. That's the reality, isn't it? If I let him get away with it, we suffer. If I don't, we suffer. There are no winners, except Charles."

"No," Augustus said. "Despite all this, Maureen, Charles isn't winning either. He'll never be happy. He never has been."

"Cry me a fucking river," she hissed. "Maybe the family is cursed. Maybe this is what they mean. Damned if we do, damned if we don't. We get to live in a hell of our own making."

Augustus wound his hand through hers. "I want you to be happy. You deserve that. What can I do for you? Anything."

Maureen leaned into him and let the rest of her tears pour out, against his chest. Several minutes passed before she answered.

"This is my cross to bear, Aggie. That I have to live with the pain while Charles never will." She looked up at him, smiling sadly. "I think I'm done with this family." She touched his cheek. "I'll be eternally grateful for what you did today. You were the only one with the courage to join me. But the others... I have to do what's best for myself and my children. I have to do what's best for my family. And that means breaking away, to a place where Charles can't hurt me anymore."

CHAPTER 18

Free Will

At first, Elizabeth hadn't thought he was going to accept. Though she'd initially fallen in love with Connor because of his inexplicable belief in everything she told him about herself, never once really questioning it, she didn't really know if he was ready to be a part of it in a more direct, meaningful way.

But Connor had taken his vows with the earnestness required, and was now a member of the Deschanel Magi Collective, an honor bestowed on non-blood only when they married into the family. He insisted he wasn't doing it simply to make her happy. That he wanted to be involved. She might never know if the truth resided on either side, or somewhere in the middle.

After, she'd kissed him and insisted she wanted to walk home. He was concerned, as anyone who loved Elizabeth had a tendency to be concerned when she did something outside her normal routine, but she kissed him again, reassuring him she was fine. More than fine. She was good. Happy. She promised him all these things, and then watched him drive away.

He'd still worry, of course. Worrying went hand in hand with loving Elizabeth Deschanel. There was nothing she could do about it, aside from remembering he chose this, and to try to alleviate as much of his anxiety over her well-being as was possible. She would do that and more, when she got home tonight. For Elizabeth had more than just a calming walk on her mind when she sent Connor on ahead.

Elizabeth fumbled in her pocket for the keys. Colin had given them to her, dropping them by in secret at The Gardens. He'd waited for the right moment and slipped them into her hands, smiling, assuring her there was no rush in getting them back. With a wink, he'd added, *hopefully you won't need to bring them back at all.*

Yes, that was the hope. And the intent. It was time, even if she was in no rush to leave their cozy apartment. It was small, but it was theirs.

But this home on Coliseum could be theirs as well. Theirs, and their children's. She wasn't pregnant yet and didn't have anything more specific than a guess as to when she would be, but it wouldn't be *too* long before Danielle came around, and Tristan only a few years later. They needed something with permanence. More so, Connor did. She could give him the gift of a strong foundation, if nothing else. A way to show him she was committed to the future, whatever was left.

Well, *she* knew what was left. But she'd never tell him. Where Elizabeth found strength in this knowledge, Connor would only find despair.

Leaving The Gardens, she skipped down Jackson, toward Coliseum. From there, it was another seven blocks to the property, which backed Lafayette Cemetery No. 1. Elizabeth didn't much like cemeteries. They reminded her of her helplessness... none more so than the one where all her loved ones were buried. But part of her new outlook involved facing her fears head-on, rather than slinking away from them in dark corners. When she sat down with the list of potential entitlement properties Colin had dropped off for her, this one stood out for that very reason. It was also close to both Colleen and Augustus, the two siblings she most needed proximity to.

When she reached the old stone walls of Lafayette No. 1, teeming with ferns and other flora peeking through the cracks, she paused. She knew the rest of the family visited the Deschanel tomb with varying levels of frequency and fervor. Mama brought flowers every week still. But unless custom dictated her presence, Elizabeth avoided the cities of death. Thousands of people were entombed in the beautifully antiquated Garden District cemetery, filling and refilling the tombs, many of which passed from family to family. But not theirs. The Deschanel tomb, which held court in the Magnolia-shaded corner of Sixth and Coliseum, was like a small city unto its own. Or a park, at least. Grass, benches, and even a small fence welcomed visitors.

Elizabeth wondered how many other places in the world viewed cemeteries as a tourist attraction. Mama often lamented that she could never get privacy with Maddy and August, because of all the "lookie-loos" huddled around their family's place of rest. Elizabeth, who had an unusual relationship with death, was curious about the world's morbid fascination with it. It was the same thing, she supposed, as people who flocked toward killers or tragedies.

Against her better judgment, she turned toward the cemetery. The tomb had been reopened for Evangeline's friend Cassie in the spring, and there were laws around opening it again so soon, so there was a kerfuffle when Lisette died. But Charles had thrown a fit, in typical Charles fashion, and Augustus calmly smoothed it over, and so Lisette, too, had been sent to her final rest without observing the required waiting period.

The cemetery was closed at this late hour, close to two in the morning, but she'd always been a good climber.

Elizabeth shoved her hands deep in her pockets as she carefully stepped over the upturned ground, dodging tree roots and cracked cement. She was alone for the first time here, and she almost missed the solemn milling about of bodies as they examined the tombs that were so uniquely New Orleans.

She rounded corner after corner, meandering through the

light fog descending. She was so lost in her thoughts that when she saw the man she had an immediate inclination to believe she was imagining it.

But no. There *was* a man. And he was kneeling at the base of the Deschanel tomb, head bowed. In his hand was a single red rose, which he placed in the concrete vase.

She recognized this man. She *knew* him. And this only confirmed a suspicion she'd held since Paris, that just because they couldn't see him, didn't mean he wasn't there. Of course he was there! He crept around in the twilight hours, haunting evenings while they slept. He visited their tomb when it was dead to the world.

Elizabeth freed her hands from her pockets and started to run. She resisted calling his name—*Tristan! Tristan!*—because instinct promised her he'd run. He didn't come here, at this hour, for confrontation, but solitude. He'd seen her future, but apparently not this moment, where it was them and only them, and she had so many questions!

Tristan perked. Twitched, like a dog picking up a scent. With a slight movement of his head, he caught her in his peripheral. And just like that, cape carrying like a wave on the wind, he bolted.

This time she did call his name. "Tristan! Wait! Please!" Elizabeth darted after him, weaving through the maze he'd created as he scaled tombs, his cloak catching the air with each leap.

He was fast, too fast for her, but she didn't slow, didn't relent. Elizabeth pressed herself as hard as she could, losing him at almost every turn but always finding him again, a snap of darkness against the moonlight.

Elizabeth needed to stop, to catch her breath, but if she did, she'd lose him. She knew it. She pushed on, her heavy breaths unfurling before her in the crisp winter air. When she came around to a dead end, she spun around, searching for any sign of him.

At last, she caught that peak of darkness, but only as it disappeared over the wall, and back into the sleeping Garden District.

Elizabeth doubled over. Her ragged breaths pulled at the air, stifled by her disappointment. Tristan. Here! He was really here, just as she always suspected. Watching over them. Over her.

But you aren't meant to meet again, Elizabeth. You know this.

Her words, her dialect, but Tristan's soothing dulcet tones.

Take comfort in knowing he's here. Whoever he is. Whatever he is. Let that be enough.

"Enough," Elizabeth whispered, mopping the sweat from her face. She smiled in the darkness.

She reached in her pocket for the keys, giving them a comforting pat, and went about climbing her way back out.

"I DON'T CARE ABOUT YOUR BASTARDS RUNNING around without a care to who they really are. But I'm concerned about yet another child in the world who could later come back and threaten everything you've built for the children you *did* want."

Charles swirled his pasta on his plate, jaw clenched. But it wasn't Cordelia he was angry with. For perhaps the first time in his life, he was angry at himself, for his own actions. He was drawing the logical line between cause and effect, and the results were painful.

"I've given that bitch so much money," he muttered. "So much."

"Well, she's too far along to get rid of the runt anyway," Cordelia said, with a delicate bite of her spaghetti. "Frankly, I'm surprised you let her live."

This whipped Charles out of his sulk. "Sorry?"

"Well, you killed her husband, so why not her?" Cordelia dropped her fork and gave him a knowing look. "Oh, come on, Charles. It's me. Why, even now, do we have to pretend you don't know what I'm talking about? Haven't I proven my loyalty to you by now?"

Charles flailed around in his inability to find a suitable comeback. The children were spending the weekend at Irish Colleen's, and he appreciated that his wife had at least waited until it was only them to approach this conversation, despite his lack of readiness for it.

"I don't need your formal acknowledgment. But I would appreciate, at least, some acceptance of how well I've kept your secrets."

"You sure ran your mouth about Ekatherina."

"Oh, please, Lisette didn't believe it. And it was fun to see her little tiny face shocked. Don't you think?"

Charles resisted a smile. The sweet naiveté of Lisette had worn off quicker than he wanted, and he, too, sometimes liked poking holes in it. He set his own fork down, having given up on finding his appetite. "I don't get it."

"Get what?"

"How you... know... how you *think* you know all these things."

"That you're a stone cold killer?"

"Fuck's sake, can you keep it down?"

"You think Richard and Condoleezza don't know?"

"There are others on staff."

"Whom you pay exceptionally well to not care," Cordelia countered. "And to answer your question, it wasn't so hard. I'm no *witch*, like some of you. I figured everything out the old-fashioned way."

Charles crossed his arms and leaned back in his chair. He could've gone his whole life never having this conversation, but now that it was here, he had to admit, he was fucking goddamn curious about the woman he'd made his wife and her almost supernatural ability to suss out the worst of him. "All right. Go on."

Cordelia took a sip of her wine. Smiled. "All right, then. That teacher. Evers. This one's easy, because all of New Orleans knew about it. Not right away, of course. It took some time for the rumor mill to catch up, and it only happened after they found the man. Everyone speculated it was your name and money that turned the police off your scent, but, of course, they don't know what your brother can do."

Charles poured another glass of cognac. Waited.

"The degenerates who hurt Evangeline were a little harder to connect, but not much. My father was the one who found out about what happened to her. If you must know, I think he was buying cocaine from some of that crowd, but he heard about the runaways who assaulted Evangeline and when he told me, I remembered something I'd read in the news. I went down to the library, to confirm my memory, and I was right. Not that a house fire is uncommon in those worn-down, forgotten neighborhoods, but it was awfully convenient how all their escapes were magically blocked off."

"They got off easy."

Cordelia's face lit up. "Yes, they did. All right, and then there's... oh yes, Colleen's professor. Well, her fall from grace at Tulane is no secret. She was wronged, as women often are in these situations. When I heard he'd driven his car into the bayou, well, I thought, this isn't the action of a man who continuously gets his way in life. And I considered the timing as well, that it happened *after* Colleen left for Scotland. When she was far enough away she'd never hear the news. Has she ever? Figured it out?"

Charles paused. Then shook his head. "Not to my knowledge."

"Good. Better that way," Cordelia said, nodding. "Now, Ekatherina was tougher. I had no evidence, or honestly, any reasons to suspect you of anything, despite your history. Women die from childbed complications all the time, as Lisette did... and no, I know you didn't kill *her*. We weren't even home. But, Ekatherina, she'd broken your brother. I know how that ate at you. Truly, it was a guess." She winked. "A very lucky guess, as it turned out. That one took some real balls."

Charles shifted in his seat. Of all of them, this weighed heaviest. But he was absolutely certain that had the woman lived, she would've run his brother right into the earth. Charles would have to visit him at the family tomb. He didn't need to be a seer to figure that out.

"Then there was the matter of Catherine."

Charles stiffened. "I told you—"

"The affair. Her strange disappearance. Again, just a guess, at least at first. But I checked with the hospitals in Boston, and there was never any record of Carolina Sullivan giving birth in any of them. Funny, that. Of course, she could have used a midwife, but with her issues? She'd want a doctor present. Yet on the same date listed on their birth announcement for Robyn, there was a Kitty Chanel who *did* give birth. To a daughter. And I thought, well Kitty... Cat... Chanel... Deschanel. Wishful thinking on her part, seeing as you were already shackled to me and she didn't have the courage to leave her own pathetic husband. And also not entirely too clever. Jane Doe would have even been better."

"Oh, Jesus. Robyn isn't Cat's. Are you crazy?"

Cordelia just looked at him.

"She wasn't pregnant when she left New Orleans. I would know." Charles' mouth turned to cotton. He tried to swallow and choked.

"Oh? Well, my mistake then." Cordelia finished her wine and poured another glass. "The others, well... Soren... the Fontaine man... those have your stamp all over them, don't they?"

"Where are you going with this? For years, you've been making these allegations, and I can't, for the life of me, figure out why, unless you want to hold them over my head."

Cordelia balked. "Isn't it obvious? I admire you. You might say I'm a fan of your work."

"Don't mock me."

"I'm better at that when that's my intention, Charles." She

sighed. "We have an interesting marriage, the two of us. Not what either of us had in mind, I suppose, but it's served its purpose. You've never loved me, but you need me. I can say the same for you. But in our own way, we do love one another, don't we? Love comes in many forms."

"So, what, you want us to kill people together?"

Cordelia laughed. "That's really your forte, not mine, dear. No, I want us to talk openly. I want you to feel free to be yourself with me, as you've never been able to with anyone, not even your Cat. I want you to know this part of you is safe with me. You'll never accuse me of tenderness, but if I ever betray your confidence, you have my permission to kill me, as you have all the others."

Charles smirked. "I wouldn't need your permission."

"No," she agreed. "But I'm giving it all the same. We are who we are, Charles. Monsters, both of us. But doesn't it sound even a little bit enticing to be monsters together?"

When Charles didn't answer, she placed one bony hand over his. "Because of you, our family is untouchable. I'm the only person in this world who will not only not judge what you've done," she said, dropping her voice to a whisper, "but will also beg you to never stop."

CHAPTER 19

The Heir

Charles looked back and forth between his brother and his best friend, calculating their anticipated reactions. They were similar creatures, Augustus and Colin, but they were not the same. Augustus did better in the abstract than he liked others to think, where Colin would follow a tunnel to the end of the world if the path made sense.

But these were the two best men he knew, hands down. And if there was anyone capable of helping him with what he now needed, it was them.

He laid out his proposal, trying his best to sound as reasonable as possible. He was very rarely accused of such a thing, and he needed them to see him this way now, or they'd spend the rest of dinner trying to talk him off the ledge.

His ask was simple.

While he built his businesses and expanded their empire, he wanted these men to raise his son.

"Well, Nicolas already stays with us during the week," Augustus said, sipping his soup. Colin tensed beside him. Colin understood that wasn't what Charles meant, even if Augustus was slow to the same realization. "It's really no trouble. Ana's happier when he's around."

"Well, *I* wasn't happy about it, at first," Charles said slowly. "Until I understood how good it was for him."

"You didn't need to call us to dinner for this, Charles. Barbara and Ana both love having him around. I love having him around. There's no problem with us continuing the arrangement."

"Charles," Colin started, coming around to the question Charles expected. "What role are you looking to play in your son's life?"

"Nicolas *will* one day be the heir," Charles said carefully. Even now, all these years later, there were times when he still got the twitch. The call for a calming whiff of that sweet white powder. "But he has to be ready for it when the time comes, in a way I wasn't. I want his upbringing guided by good men, who will show him how to become a good man."

Colin and Augustus exchanged a look, but neither of them corrected him. Neither reassured Charles that *he* was a good man.

But he didn't come here for that. He came here to secure his son's future.

"What are you asking, exactly?" Augustus pressed.

"That you both treat him as your own son." Charles almost choked on his own words. "He doesn't need money, he needs guidance. He needs to know right from wrong. He needs to be accountable in a way..." He drained his glass. "He needs more, okay? He needs more."

"Oz and Nicolas are inseparable," Colin answered. "I see no reason for that to change. And I know he's very close with Ana."

"Thick as thieves," Augustus answered.

"But what about the girls?" Colin asked. "They don't even have their mother around now."

Charles could have smacked him for talking so lightly about this topic in public, but what did it even matter anymore? Of course the whole fucking city knew those kids hadn't come from Cordelia. Nothing a Deschanel had ever done was theirs for safe-keeping anymore.

"Cordelia has changed," Charles said, though he didn't think his wife had changed so much as adapted. She wasn't caring for his daughters out of any warmth or nostalgia but need. They needed a mother, and so she stepped into the role. But what would that mean? What would they learn from a woman with ice running through her veins?

But was Irish Colleen any better, replacing tenderness for pragmatism?

"She's good with them," he went on, more for himself. "In our family, it was the boys who struggled. Don't fight me on this, Augustus. Both of us suffered without a father."

Augustus said nothing.

"We had to figure out for ourselves how to be a man. We didn't have uncles to guide us, either. We had nothing," Charles said. "I'm shifting my focus to the business side of things. For too long, Deschanels have enjoyed the spoils without understanding how to build them further. I want an empire for my son. For my daughters."

"You keep saying that word," Colin said. "Empire. But you have one, Charles. Your predecessors saw to that, and you have entire teams at your disposal who exist solely to protect and grow it. Do you even know how much your net worth grows by the day? By the second? On interest alone?"

"And how do I get to feel good about that, huh? When I had no hand in it? How do I look my son in the eye and hand him the keys to a kingdom I had no help in building?"

"If it's that important to you..."

"It is," Charles asserted.

"All right, then," Colin said, turning toward Augustus with a somewhat bewildered look. "Should the two of us grab lunch sometime this week, then? We can talk about a rotation, if that works?"

Augustus nodded. Charles couldn't read him. "I'll check my calendar before we all leave tonight."

"Good. Good," Colin said, nodding, as if they'd just

completed a successful, albeit unusual, business transaction. "So, Augustus, tell me about Barbara. She seems lovely."

Charles smiled to himself and let the men make their small talk. He had no time for it. No time for small *anything* anymore.

His son was secure.

His daughters were secure, for now.

He could take care of the rest. Building something with his own hands, his own *smarts.* The family joke about how many years Charles spent in college would die away, replaced by whispers of his incredible prowess as an entrepreneur. His shrewd mind for business. He didn't need to understand any of it to turn it into something.

None of the rest mattered. Not anymore.

Charles had a future to tend to, and there was no one better suited for the task than a man who existed happily only when he existed in the extremes.

MAUREEN WAS STARTLED AT HOW OLD HER MOTHER had become while Maureen was dealing with her own troubles. She wasn't yet fifty, but sat hunched like an old woman. Years later, she would look back on this moment and remember that there were signs, even then.

"I know what Charles did. What he's done," Irish Colleen said, after Maureen told her, stumbling over her words, that after Christmas she'd be taking some space from the family. All except her mother, that was. "I've always known."

Maureen recoiled. She'd said nothing about Charles in her heartfelt outpouring. "What do you mean, Mama?"

"Oh, darling." Irish Colleen closed her eyes, pulling the afghan over her shoulders. "All of you, always, have thought me a fool. Because I'm not like you. Because I don't understand what it's like to be like you."

"I don't think that, Mama," Maureen said, feeling shame in her lie. She had once thought Irish Colleen to be a great fool, but now, a mother of her own, she understood better. She understood all too well.

"Maybe not now, but you did. You all did. But I saw a lot more than you think. I know who my oldest son is, Maureen Amelia. And though I wished he could change, wished he could grow to be more like his father, he never did. I watched him try, and I watched him fail." Her head fell back with a wistful look. "He does try. Charles. He does. But his trying is so much less than a good man's."

Maureen was stunned. She'd never heard her mother say anything like this about Charles before. Although Irish Colleen had chided him for his behaviors, she'd never really punished him in any meaningful way. In Maureen's eyes, Charles was the only one of them who'd ever been above the law at home, and later, the law of the world.

She remembered Edouard's words last night. They'd come on the heels of him shocking her by taking both her hands in his.

I want to do right by you, Maureen. I'm old now... older than I ever expected to be. I enjoy being a father, to both of my children, and I can appreciate that our start was auspicious. He'd shaken his head. *No, I won't do this now, when I'm trying to give you more. It was worse. I hurt you. I can't take this back, but I can give you what you wanted from me all along. I will give it to you. I'll make up for the loss created by your brother's cruelty. And I'll make your happiness a priority, from now on. You have my word.*

She didn't know who this man was who'd replaced her husband, but when he said the words, a switch flipped within her. One that pushed aside their hurtful past, replacing it with a path of bright light ahead. Only the good things were allowed there now. Only the colors that painted their happiness.

"Sweet Maureen. Your happiness is more important to me than anything in the world," Irish Colleen said. Tears trickled down her skin, which had long since lost its pliancy. Age spots colored around her eyes and mouth. "Maybe more than all the others. You're so like me. More than you'll ever know."

Maureen smiled, lowering her head to hide the tears. "Oh, I know it, Mama."

"You wrap your beautiful family in a loving cocoon, Maureen, and you hold them tight in it, until everything else fades away." Her bony hands squeezed Maureen's knee. "And you don't worry about what others think. We spend too much of our lives focusing on that and are none the happier."

Maureen sobbed into her hands. "I want that, Mama. To be happy. I want that more than anything."

Irish Colleen stood and knelt by her daughter's chair, gathering her in her arms. "And so you will be, now, my darling. So you will be."

AUGUSTUS PASSED THE BREAD BASKET ACROSS THE table to Colin.

"Thanks for meeting me on short notice, and in the middle of the holiday season. I thought it was best to get this sorted before Christmas," Colin said, tucking his napkin in his lap. "And for the excuse to eat at Mr. B's. My favorite."

"Mine as well," Augustus said. "Try to serve a good Gulf shrimp in my house, and Ana will let you have it."

Colin grinned. "Is she even from Louisiana? Maybe the stork delivered her?"

"Oh, she's a Deschanel, through and through. I'd know that temper anywhere."

"At least part of why we're here, I suppose," Colin said. He buttered his bread, but left it untouched on his plate. "You think your brother is starting to realize things about himself?"

Augustus did think this, but he knew too much about Charles now to give him a pass. Knowing what he knew changed things. This knowledge had taken such a hold on Augustus that he had half a mind to force a judge to let him adopt Nicolas. The girls, too. "Such as?"

Colin cocked his head. "Come on, Augustus. If Charles

didn't have his money, and his name, he wouldn't have many kind words said about him. You and I, we know him. We know he's better than the things he does, and we love him for who he is beyond that. But fatherhood only changed him so much. That he realizes this might be a turning point for your brother."

"For all his faults, Charles loves his children," Augustus said carefully. "On some level, some place where his ego doesn't hold so much sway, he knows they need more than he can give him."

"Whether he knows it or not, it's true. But it's good he came to us, anyway. Better for it to be his idea."

"What do you mean?"

"Well, only that I've been thinking the same thing for some time. That those kids, especially Nicolas, deserved a better father." Colin held his hands up. "Now, hear me out. I love Charles. He's my brother, too. But he's so hot and cold with the boy, and I can see it in Nicolas' eyes when he comes back after a weekend at home."

Augustus didn't have time for Colin's wishy-washy view of Charles. He'd never been willing, or able, to see Charles for who he was, and that whitewashing existed as a wall in their friendship that kept both sides happy. But it was an illusion. A lie. "How about this, then? I'll keep Nicolas during the school week and then you can have him Friday night through the weekend."

"When will Charles see him?"

"I don't know. But that's not really our concern right now, is it? We're here about Nicolas."

"I suppose so." Colin frowned, thoughtful. "So much has changed in a decade, don't you think? Ronald Reagan is going to be president next year. An actor, would you believe?"

"Maddy would be rolling in her grave."

Colin laughed. "And look at all of us. We're family men and women now, all of us. Even Chelsea is talking about having some children. But I feel compelled to mention how much Charles has changed, too, since we're here about him. About his son. He's not the man he was ten years ago, or even five."

"That's true of anyone," Augustus challenged.

"He's always been a hard man to love," Colin went on, and Augustus had the feeling he was talking more to himself. "But to love a man like Charles Deschanel is to know a man the outside world refuses to. You know, for years there were rumors, about him and my Cat. Stupid rumors. Neither one of them is capable of hurting me like that, but it didn't stop tongues from wagging in this town."

Augustus thought that if there was an Olympic sport for self-delusion, Colin would win it with flying colors, year after year. "It doesn't matter what others say."

"No," Colin said with a dreamy look. "But I always wished for a woman for Charles like Cat. Someone who could love with her passion."

Augustus was relieved when the waiter delivered their food. An excuse to stop talking, and for Colin to do the same. "Whatever he has with Cordelia, it seems to be keeping him satisfied for now."

Colin smiled sadly as he went in for a bite of his shrimp and grits. "For now."

AN HOUR LATER, AUGUSTUS HUNG HIS JACKET ON THE coat rack inside Magnolia Grace. A rich, welcoming scent wafted in from the kitchen. Gumbo, he thought, and realized once more how fortunate he was to be married to a woman like Barbara.

He followed the aroma, but she wasn't in the kitchen. "I'm home!" he called out, and the answer came from an adjoining room, their formal dining area.

Augustus found Barbara and Anasofiya huddled together over a large puzzle. Barbara had climbed half over the table to place a piece on the other side. Ana bit her lip in intense concentration. When she saw Barbara's success, she cheered, and they gave each other high-fives over the table.

Augustus cocked his head, walking around to see what they

were working on. Tower Bridge, but it was still missing part of the Thames and some blue in the beams.

"Ana picked it out," Barbara said, planting a kiss at the corner of his mouth. Ana ran over and smacked her lips against his cheek before returning to the very serious task at hand.

"You both have made fine work of it," Augustus praised. "That's a lot of pieces."

"We're going there!" Ana declared. "For our family vacation next year!"

Augustus looked at Barbara, who shrugged, but was smiling.

"You heard her," she said with a wink and went back to helping Ana assemble their masterpiece.

Augustus' eyes glossed over. He willed his tears back where they came from before they could make a formal appearance.

He didn't need them here.

Everything was as it should be, finally.

CHAPTER 20

So This is Christmas

Evangeline had hardly seen Johannes since they stepped through the threshold of The Gardens.

The moment they entered, he was swept up in a wave of curious siblings and a very serious Mama, who insisted on taking his measure early and often. As far as she knew, none of the other significant others among them had been so eagerly anticipated. Was it because she was the last to find love? Was it because she was different?

He fielded questions from all sides, and did it with a beaming smile. Her Johannes. Was there another man, or woman, on earth more perfect for her? Cassie had been, but she'd loved Cassie in a different way, and that love had healed her. Prepared her for not only this man, but this moment.

Nearly everyone hinted that it was time for them to move home. Deschanels should be together. Both Colleen—who knew the value of living away for a while—and Elizabeth defended her, the latter trying to explain to those who didn't understand the prestige in the work Evangeline was doing. There was even talk that their research team might be on the nomination list for a Nobel Prize. This was hard even for her to grasp, but her family?

She liked this middle ground, where she could be amongst

them but also away, and be herself. It was the best of both worlds, as they say, and she appreciated them more when she wasn't embroiled in their madness. This she'd slowly learned in Massachusetts, and now had come to fully embrace as an expat living abroad. Besides, she loved the simplicity and beauty of Geneva. It appealed to a mind always in chaos.

And, yeah, Evangeline thought maybe she *did* want children of her own. Even five years ago, her answer was *no fucking way*, but time and circumstances had brought her further away from the young girl drowning in New Orleans and closer to the woman who could thrive in the right environment. She'd passed from one petri dish to another, and her testing was complete. She was whole. She could share some of this with the next generation, luck willing.

"You have my blessing, for whatever that's worth," Irish Colleen said, breaking Evangeline from the spell of so many thoughts.

"Sorry, Mama?"

"Johannes. He's a fine man."

"Don't sound so surprised I was able to stick the landing on this one," Evangeline teased.

"Oh! I'm not surprised about that, Evangeline. Only that you could get past your own self long enough to be happy."

Evangeline's defenses rankled, but her mother went on.

"You have a good soul. Of all my babies, it may be the most pure, but the pure ones are the most susceptible, aren't they? You've always been my wild card. The one afraid to fail and afraid to be vulnerable."

"Not everyone can bounce back from things so easily."

"No, darling. And some hurts are meant to be felt. They give us the strength we need for whatever comes next. And the permission to enjoy it."

"I wouldn't change it, though, Mama." Evangeline looked out into the crowd of family. Of her siblings and their spouses. The small feet of many children pattering around the marble floors, running loops around the several Christmas trees and miles of garland. "I wouldn't be here now if the bad things hadn't happened."

"My private girl," Irish Colleen said, smiling. "I've always found it so hard to peek into the dark places you go."

"Oh, they're pretty dark." Evangeline laughed.

"I know you'll be fine, darling." Irish Colleen patted her arm. "Just fine."

COLLEEN STRUGGLED TO SEE THROUGH THE BLUR OF tears and tiny lights. They'd come a long way since the days Mama did her best to see to a happy Christmas for the seven of them. All of them, now, married or on the path. Eleven little grandchildren, the breath of new life and new hope, played in their velvet dresses and mini tuxedos. Saddle shoes slapped against the marble and pitched voices called across the halls as they played their games.

Ten years was both a whisper across time and an eternity.

Ten years ago, Colleen saw no future for her that didn't involve solving the problems of others. She had no room for love and light.

Ten years ago, Charles was one foot in the grave, throwing his responsibilities to the wind.

Ten years ago, Augustus existed quietly in the corners of their family, looking only to a future away from them, only to be broken by the loss of Maddy.

Ten years ago, Evangeline, the smartest of them all, struggled in school and socially, searching and failing to find her place in the world.

Ten years ago, Maureen's temperament stifled her and pushed her into places that only caused her more harm.

Ten years ago, Elizabeth was still climbing trees by day and crying herself to sleep by night.

And ten years ago, Maddy was still alive.

Colleen glanced at the clock.

Ahh, but not for long.

"You have that serious look," Noah said, handing her a glass of wine. "The one that usually involves some level of plotting."

"Not this time," Colleen replied, dabbing at her eyes. Charles and Cordelia huddled nearby, *laughing.* Connor stole a kiss from Elizabeth under the mistletoe, while, feet away, Edouard had a protective hand at Maureen's waist. Across the room, Augustus practically glowed next to his new wife, Barbara. "Only a bit reflective, that's all."

"You always accuse me of being the nostalgic one."

"That's because you are!" They both laughed. "But there's a time and place for it, even for an old pragmatist like me."

"Old." Noah wrinkled his nose. "Don't count us out just yet. We're still spry spring chickens, lass."

Colleen reached one hand toward her lower back, wincing. "Speak for yourself, Jameson."

Noah wrapped his arm around her waist, pulling her in. "I'll give it a wee rub later."

Colleen rested her head against his shoulder. "Keep talking in that terrible Scottish brogue and there might be something in it for you."

Elizabeth buried her hands in the soapy sink, feeling around for the rogue silverware at the bottom. Beside her, her mother worked at drying and putting away the finished ones. They cleaned up together in silence, waiting as the others brought in more dishes from the dinner.

"I like Johannes," Irish Colleen ventured.

"He's perfect for Evie." Elizabeth felt around until she grabbed a handful of something. "I think they'll be very happy together."

"A guess or a premonition?"

"I don't know, Mama. I haven't seen anything bad for them. But that doesn't mean..."

"Yes, darling, I know." Irish Colleen stopped for a moment, bracing herself against the counter. "You've changed, you know."

Elizabeth answered without looking up. "Have I?"

"I can't put my finger on it. It could be married life, I suppose." Irish Colleen turned back to drying, nodding to herself. "Yes, it could be that."

"Maybe it's that. Maybe it's the Council. I'm glad you see it," Elizabeth said. Their entire relationship, most of her life, had been predicated on an amalgam of her mother's fussiness over her well-being and anachronistic reliance on the same visions that caused her harm. That her mother could acknowledge this change was almost more important to her than her own self-reflection on the matter.

"I do, Lizzy. If you're happy, that's all I ever wanted for you. For any of you."

"I think we're all as happy as we can be," Elizabeth replied. "Even Charles, in his own way."

"For Charles, happiness will always involve some degree of illusion," Irish Colleen replied. "But we all find our way through, don't we?"

"Yes, Mama."

"And you know your old mother has to ask... when will it be my Lizzy's turn to give me grandbabies?"

The old Elizabeth would have tensed up at the latest of her mother's inappropriate expectations on her. But frustration had no place here, between them, in what would be, Elizabeth now knew, the last decade of her mother's life.

So, she smiled. "Soon, Mama. For Christmas, I delivered the keys to the Coliseum house to Connor. That feels like a good first step in that direction, wouldn't you say?"

"Oh, what a wonderful choice! I always loved that house. Very close to our old one, you know."

"I know, Mama."

"You'll make beautiful memories there together, Lizzy. I know it."

For a while, yes. "Mama, I want you to know... I want you to know that I love you, and you did the best you could with the seven of us. It wasn't easy to begin with, and we didn't make it easier on you. But all of us are going to be okay, and it all started with a mama who loved us through the best and worst of who we were."

Irish Colleen set her towel aside, hunched over the counter. When Elizabeth pulled her mother in for a hug, she saw she was crying.

"My Lizzy," she whispered, drying her tears on her youngest daughter's Christmas dress.

"My Mama," Elizabeth returned and, pulling back, looked her mother in the eye and smiled. "Now, let's go see Maddy."

Epilogue: Irish Colleen and the Seven

Colleen Deschanel, known as Irish Colleen to her family and friends, walked past her seven children and eleven grandchildren, as she did every night of her life.

But tonight was different. It was unlike any that had come before.

It had been Elizabeth's idea, but she'd met no objections from any of them.

Irish Colleen's entire brood huddled together at Lafayette Cemetery No. 1 just after midnight. The cemetery was closed at this hour, but Elizabeth had wiggled over the wall, opening one of the gates that locked from the inside. Irish Colleen was nervous about breaking the law, but when no one else batted an eyelash, she realized her worries had no place.

She'd never learned the exact time of Madeline's death. The information was available, but it didn't matter, because had Maddy died, for her, in the long, arduous seconds between the police arriving at her door and them delivering the news, words she would die thinking about. Much of her had died then, with her daughter. But curling up and rotting away was no option for Irish Colleen, who had six other children who needed her.

But had she seen herself surviving to the ten-year anniversary of this terrible event?

She had not.

But it was, nonetheless, the ten-year anniversary of the seven becoming six.

But they weren't six, either. They were seventeen. More if you counted the spouses. If you counted Irish Colleen.

And they were all there, whether you counted them or not. Children. Spouses. And of course, Irish Colleen, who never thought of herself as a matriarch but had been called that several times just that night, by all of her children.

There was a chill in the midwinter air. Everyone waited for someone else to start talking, but they weren't a family known for their words, but their strength.

The strong shall rise again, Elizabeth had said, earlier, reminding her of the family motto of August's people. Irish Colleen never thought much about this. As an Irishwoman, everything had meaning, and so nothing did. But it was true, wasn't it? Didn't the Deschanels always rise again?

Each of them milled around, lost to their thoughts, shuffling over the dead grass.

Charles stood with Cordelia, three of their girls standing at their legs while they hovered at the corner of the tomb in shared silence. Adrienne slept in a buggy that Cordelia mindlessly rocked back and forth. Nicolas was elsewhere.

With Augustus, she realized, as her eyes fell on her second son. She'd always seen him as the darkness to Charles' light, but only lately realized she'd mistaken darkness for the shadows of others brighter than him. Had she done right, pairing him with the Chandler girl? Yes, she thought, she had. Ana looked up at her father and stepmother, curious, each of her hands clutched in one of each of theirs.

Colleen held Ashley, while Noah held tight to Amelia and Ben. Colleen cried as she traced her fingers over Maddy's etched name. Noah held fast to her side, her silent, stalwart strength.

Evangeline stood off in the corner, pressed against the picket fence that was supposed to make visitors feel welcome. Johannes was behind her, and she leaned into him with a pensive look toward the tomb.

Maureen was on her knees at the base of it, Edouard standing protectively behind her as she sobbed. He held Alain tight to his breast, while Olivia knelt by her mother, catching the contagion of her sorrow.

And Lizzy.

She sat upon one of the benches, watching them all in silence, Connor bowed over at her side.

"I was going to bring some music," she said, cutting a strange tear in the calm. "Maddy, if nothing else, had pretty boss taste in tunes."

Small ripples of laughter tittered through the family, interlaced with sniffles and sighs.

"And then I thought about making a speech, but she didn't really have much time for words, did she? She was all about action."

Augustus pulled a hand to his mouth, trapping a sob there. Barbara ran a hand down his back.

"Maddy wanted to save the world. Instead, in her own way, she saved all of us." Elizabeth raised an invisible glass, eyes traveling across the huddle of everyone who mattered. "For Maddy."

Amidst sniffles and soft sobs, everyone else slowly raised their own arms into the air.

"For Maddy," they repeated, out of unison, the words bouncing around and through them as they each found their voices.

"For Maddy," Irish Colleen called, louder than them all. Louder than the pain, louder than the joy. Louder than the memories. Louder than her faults. "For The Seven."

. . .

Author's Note: Read on for Beyond the Seven, a glimpse into the intervening years between The Seven and The House of Crimson & Clover.

Looking for more *Crimson & Clover* to soothe the book hangover?

The House of Crimson & Clover: Present day. The Seven are all in their middle ages now, and their children are stepping into their own adult lives. But sinister curses and ancient foes have slept for too long, and the battle their parents never needed to fight has now become theirs to own. Start with ***The Storm and the Darkness***.

Vampires of the Merovingi: Etienne de Blanchefort knows he's being watched. Worse, he knows his specter isn't human. Let this historical fantasy, set initially in the tropics of Saint-Domingue, whisk you away in ***The Island.***

Or, read on for Beyond the Seven

Beyond the Seven

Narratively, there is a twenty-six-year gap between The Seven Series and the next chronological tale in the universe, *The Storm and the Darkness*, the prequel tale that starts The House of Crimson & Clover Series. If you'd like to know what happens to the characters during this gap (much of which is told in retrospect in The House of Crimson & Clover Series), please read on for some of the highlights. These are not spoilers so much as a bridge of information that takes you from one series to the next, though if you prefer to discover these fates through the piecing together of information in the later series, now is the time to stop reading.

Still reading? First, it's important you know, 1996 was a *very* rough year for everyone in the family, thanks to the Deschanel Curse finally descending upon them.

Prefer to find out for yourself? Continue on with ***The Storm and the Darkness***.

Otherwise...

After 1980...

Charles

The tenuous truce between Charles and Cordelia eventually, over time, erodes away, driven by Cordelia's resentment of Charles' absence in his daughters' lives, in addition to his madness taking deeper hold. Her anger at Charles turns to cold malice, which she directs at the four girls. Cordelia's behavior also drives a wedge between Charles and the only son he will ever have, Nicolas, who eventually returns home to live at Ophélie and is inadvertently used as a pawn in their marriage wars. When Charles' youngest, Adrienne, turns sixteen, in 1996, she begins a clandestine relationship with Colin and Catherine's son, Oz, who is five years her senior. This relationship becomes the catalyst for Charles' decision to take his family away from New Orleans for the summer, a decision which proves fatal. On the drive, Charles loses control of the car and he, Cordelia, and his three oldest daughters are killed in an accident. Adrienne's body isn't found at the scene, and her story is told in a Crimson & Clover Lagniappe, *St. Charles at Dusk*. Nicolas was not in the car, having not been invited, and is left, at twenty-one, to deal with the loss of his entire family. The secret of Charles and Catherine's child, Robyn, remains buried.

Further reading:

Nicolas' story begins— *The Storm and the Darkness* (The House of Crimson & Clover Series)

The story of Adrienne & Oz— *St. Charles at Dusk* (Crimson & Clover Lagniappes Series)

Short story about Giselle— *Banshee* (Crimson & Clover Lagniappes Series)

Short story about Anne Fontaine (Charles' daughter with Angelique)— *Flourish* (Crimson & Clover Lagniappes Series)

Augustus

Augustus becomes even more immersed in his work, relying on Barbara to raise Anasofiya while he takes his business global. He loves Ana beyond words, but is afraid of failing her the way he feels he's failed both Madeline and Ekatherina. He fears Anasofiya will have similar predilections toward the macabre, like her mother. He focuses on what he can control—building a company he can one day leave to his only child. Anasofiya struggles to connect with others, but is not like her mother. She's brave and thoughtful, and her close relationship with her cousin, Nicolas, is her lifeline.

Further reading:

Anasofiya's story begins— *The Storm and the Darkness* (The House of Crimson & Clover Series)

Short story about Anasofiya and Oz— *Surrender* (Crimson & Clover Lagniappes Series)

Short story about Jonathan St. Andrews & Summer Island— *Shame* (Crimson & Clover Lagniappes Series)

Colleen

Colleen and Noah raise their three children—Amelia, Ben, and Ashley—in New Orleans, as both Colleen's and Noah's medical careers take on new heights. As magistrate, Colleen grows further into her role as family leader smoothly and naturally, breathing new life into the tradition. Amelia, her oldest, becomes a powerful empath, which makes connections with others challenging and painful. She goes to school for psychology. Benjamin marries his high school sweetheart, Laurel, and they have one son, Colby. And Ashley, an elementalist who can conjure storms when his emotions are heightened, also marries, a woman named Christine, with whom he has three children—Alexander, Benjamin, and Katey. Ashley pours his energies into a career in finance, having no time for the world his mother leads. In 1996, tragedy strikes Colleen's family as well. Benjamin, his wife, and child are killed in a tragic house fire.

Further reading:

The beginning of The House of Crimson & Clover— *The Storm and the Darkness* (The House of Crimson & Clover Series. Colleen and her children make their biggest appearances several books in)

Short story about how Colleen and Noah met— *A Band of Heather* (Crimson & Clover Lagniappes Series. This story is, however, mostly redundant to the story told in The Seven)

Evangeline

Evangeline and Johannes Gehring go on to have two children, Markus and Katja. They eventually leave Switzerland and return to the States, though not to New Orleans. Evangeline and Johannes, both revered scientists after their time at CERN and their short-listing for a Nobel Prize, are hired on as nuclear physicists at the Pentagon, in Washington, D.C, where they settle down to raise their family and build a long-term life. The children are very similar to the parents: sharp, resolved, focused.

Further reading:

The beginning of The House of Crimson & Clover— *The Storm and the Darkness* (The House of Crimson & Clover Series. Evangeline and her children make their biggest appearances several books in)

Maureen

Maureen's husband, Edouard, eventually passes away in 1998. Before that point, he lived up to his promise to, in his own way, be a better husband to her, and, in her own way, she was happy. She brings her children up to be fearful and distrusting of all things magic. Maureen's estrangement from her family makes her instruction stick, as there are no outside influences to show the children who they are and where they've come from. She never does reconnect with the dead. Olivia marries a nice, dependable man, Greg, and they have one child, Rory. Alain is not married.

Further reading:

The beginning of The House of Crimson & Clover— *The Storm and the Darkness* (The House of Crimson & Clover Series. Maureen and her children make their biggest appearances several books in)

Elizabeth

Elizabeth and Connor have two children in the eighties. First, Danielle, and then, Tristan. Elizabeth's visions become even more problematic for her, despite her newfound wisdom, which drives a wedge in her marriage, leaving Connor helpless to know how to soothe something he can never fix. In 1996, Elizabeth loses what's left of her resolve when the first of her terrible visions come true and Danielle is hit by a car and killed. She retreats into herself, leaving Connor and Tristan confused and alone, as the hour of her own death approaches.

Further reading:

The beginning of The House of Crimson & Clover— *The Storm and the Darkness* (The House of Crimson & Clover Series. Elizabeth and her children make their biggest appearances several books in)

Irish Colleen

Irish Colleen lives out her remaining days in her suite at The Gardens, enjoying her life as a grandmother. In 1990, she passes away peacefully after a quiet and prolonged illness. Mercifully, Irish Colleen does not live to see the deaths that sweep her family and dies believing everything was just as it should be. *1980* is Irish

Colleen's last appearance in any Saga of Crimson & Clover series, as of this publication.

The Sullivans

Colin and Catherine stay married and raise Oz to be a serious, responsible young man, who eventually goes on to join the firm with his father. Rory and Carolina raise their three children, including the one they secretly adopted from Catherine, happily, with Cameron and Robyn going on to become lawyers as well. Clancy dates Anasofiya in high school, and then eventually goes on to enjoy a successful career outside law. Robyn and Cameron both have children of their own. Patrick and Isabella have twins, Quillan and Riley, while Chelsea and her husband, Mason, have triplets—Dylan, Kieran, and Kelly, who are just as mischievous as their mother. The family remains close to the Deschanels, both personally and professionally.

Further reading:

The story of Adrienne & Oz— *St. Charles at Dusk* (Crimson & Clover Lagniappes Series)

The Sullivan lives continue to mix with the Deschanels— *The Storm and the Darkness* (The House of Crimson & Clover Series)

Short story about Anasofiya and Oz— *Surrender* (Crimson & Clover Lagniappes Series)

Short story about Chelsea Landry's Triplets— *Dark Blessing* (Crimson & Clover Lagniappes Series)

Short story about Autumn Sullivan (a cousin to Oz)— *The Ephemeral* (Crimson & Clover Lagniappes Series)

Ready to start The House of Crimson & Clover? Download ***The Storm and the Darkness*** and you won't miss a beat.

Also by Sarah M. Cradit

KINGDOM OF THE WHITE SEA

Kingdom of the White Sea Trilogy

The Kingless Crown

The Broken Realm

The Hidden Kingdom

The Book of All Things

Blackwood Cycle

The Raven and the Rush

The Poison and the Paladin

Southerlands Cycle

The Sylvan and the Sand

The Flame and the Forsaken

Guardians Cycle

The Altruist and the Assassin

The Belle and the Blackbird

Darkwood Cycle

The Melody and the Master

The Hand and the Heart

Sceptre Cycle

The Claw and the Crowned

The Duke and the Disciple

THE SAGA OF CRIMSON & CLOVER

<u>The House of Crimson and Clover Series</u>

The Storm and the Darkness

Shattered

The Illusions of Eventide

Bound

Midnight Dynasty

Asunder

Empire of Shadows

Myths of Midwinter

The Hinterland Veil

The Secrets Amongst the Cypress

Within the Garden of Twilight

House of Dusk, House of Dawn

<u>Midnight Dynasty Series</u>

A Tempest of Discovery

A Storm of Revelations

A Torrent of Deceit

<u>The Seven Series</u>

Nineteen Seventy

Nineteen Seventy-Two

Nineteen Seventy-Three

Nineteen Seventy-Four

Nineteen Seventy-Five

Nineteen Seventy-Six

Nineteen Eighty

Vampires of the Merovingi Series

The Island

and more

The Dusk Trilogy

St. Charles at Dusk: The Story of Oz and Adrienne

Flourish: The Story of Anne Fontaine

Banshee: The Story of Giselle Deschanel

Crimson & Clover Stories

Available as a single collection, The Shorts

Surrender: The Story of Oz and Ana

Shame: The Story of Jonathan St. Andrews

Fire & Ice: The Story of Remy & Fleur

Dark Blessing: The Landry Triplets

Pandora's Box: The Story of Jasper & Pandora

The Menagerie: Oriana's Den of Iniquities

A Band of Heather: The Story of Colleen and Noah

The Ephemeral: The Story of Autumn & Gabriel

Bayou's Edge: The Landry Triplets

For more information, and exciting bonus material, visit www.sarahmcradit.com

About the Author

Sarah is the USA Today and International Bestselling Author of over forty contemporary and epic fantasy stories, and the creator of the Kingdom of the White Sea and Saga of Crimson & Clover universes.

Born a geek, Sarah spends her time crafting rich and multilayered worlds, obsessing over history, playing her retribution paladin (and sometimes destruction warlock), and settling provocative Tolkien debates, such as why the Great Eagles are not Gandalf's personal taxi service. Passionate about travel, she's been to over twenty countries collecting sparks of inspiration, and is always planning her next adventure.

Sarah and her husband live in a beautiful corner of SE Pennsylvania with their three tiny benevolent pug dictators.

www.sarahmcradit.com